Tender Nightmare

by
Ray E. Spencer

Writers Club Press
San Jose · New York · Lincoln · Shanghai

Tender Nightmare
Copyright © 1999 by Ray E. Spencer

ISBN: 1-893652-45-9

LCCN: 99-64071

Published by Writers Club Press, an imprint of iUniverse.com, Inc.

For information address:
iUniverse.com, Inc.
620 North 48th Street
Suite 201
Lincoln, NE 68504-3467
www.iuniverse.com

URL: http://www.writersclub.com

To the Lord our God for giving me the ability to write and the love of reading.

To Bonnie, my loving wife. To my loving son, Raymond. To my loving growing-up family: Dad (Richard), Mom (Alice), Jan, Rich, Bob (my twin), and Sherm. Thank you all for your love and support.

Introduction

In 1954, humans, on the average, weren't supposed to meet their Maker until after the sixty-eighth anniversary of their birth.

This tale may be hard to believe; then again, maybe it's not. It was told to me by one of the participants, Timothy—a *dear* friend, with such vividness that I feel as if I had been present when the events unfolded. I'm a Red Sox fan; you, the reader, need not know my name.

The storytelling begins after the first day of classes at the local elementary school in Saint Petersburg, a resort town in west central Florida. Timothy's family was just one of many trying to carve out a calm and fruitful existence in a nice place.

But death, evil death, came as powerful opponent.

Chapter 1

"Aren't you scared, huh?" Tim Tender said to his twin brother.

"No, man. But, it's a monster alright. And look at the way the weather over the years has beaten it up," Todd returned, pointing his right forefinger toward the two-story, white with broken red shutters, decayed dwelling on Chimera Road.

"I'm not sure we should even go in the place," Tim said as a worried look developed on his slender face.

"Check out all the damn screens on the ground around the house," Dink said. Dink Playlen was also a twin; his sibling's name was Link—unlike Todd and Tim, they were physical duplicates.

"Yes, with mesh spikes sticking up waiting for some shoeless kid to come along," Tim added. He walked forward and stood next to a sign. "Check this out—'Keep Out, No Entry'—like metal guard dogs watching over their master's residence. I'm not going in there."

"Don't be such a sissy," Dink replied.

"We need a clubhouse. Remember, Tim, your sweetie, Miss Tester, suggested we start a club." Todd had a playful grin on his mug. "So, we need a place where nobody will bother us."

Tim Tender had a crush on the fifth-grade teacher, Annie Tester, at Lakeside Elementary, where the two sets of twins had just completed the initial Monday of their sixth- grade, big-shot year.

"Stuff it! She's not my sweetie."

"It's four-thirty, fourteen minutes to the start of the meeting, and Link must still be in the principal's office. Do you think he'll get swats?" Dink asked his best friends.

"Of course," Todd said, "doesn't everybody?"

"The Barrens were all killed in that dungeon, huh? Look at the Spanish moss hanging from the oak trees...the scene reminds me of recently-executed prisoners," Tim said. He, as well as his four-minute-older relative, read books like other people smoked cigarettes: one right after the other. Tim loved words.

"That was three years ago! Do you think their ghosts are running around in there?" Dink's sarcasm couldn't be held back.

"They might be! The way they were killed—dismembering their bodies and sewing the arms, legs, and heads back on in different places than where they came from...gruesome," Tim shook his face, as if trying to discard the image from his brain.

"Yea, man, the law couldn't tell who was the father or son or mother or daughter—two combinations of each. Weird, very weird," Todd said.

"The only one not chopped up was Mother Barren's uncle from Warsaw," Dink added. "Maybe he should have stayed in Poland."

One overcast, muggy night in '51, the whole Barren lineage was extinguished, supposedly by an inmate from Saint Petersburg's mental ward, Saint Sid's, which rested behind the Barren clan's residence. The hospital had a steel chain-link fence with three feet of cutting-edge barbed wire at its top, enclosing the building. There had always been a question around town as to how anyone could have managed the climb. After the dreadful incident, the hospital staff kept the scapegoat under lock and key.

The medical examiner had suggested that the family members did not become corpses via the cutting ceremony; instead, were dead as a result of direct injections of hydrogen peroxide into their hearts. There were other curious things: at the end of the two kid-sized right arms, the hands were lacking the thumbs and forefingers, and the missing body parts were never located.

The three boys advanced like babies just learning to walk toward the seven steps leading up to the grotesque-looking mansion.

"Man, look at the front doors," Todd said, as he pointed toward the recessed entryway.

"Double doors, so what?" Dink said.

"I see what you mean," Tim responded, "the word, *Usher*, is etched on each side. I think that's an omen, let's get out of here." His feet were retreating.

"No, we can't; we need a place to conduct the meetings of the newly-elected officials of the soon-to-be-famous T&P club. What kind of wood is that, Dink?" Todd asked.

"Cherry-wood!" Dink said as he tested it with a closed fist. His uncle Stephen, who managed King's Furniture Store downtown, had taught him about different types of wood and the trees that spawned them.

"So, let me get this straight...you're President, Todd; Dink's Sergeant at Arms; I'm Secretary/Treasurer; and Link, is the VP, correct?"

"You got it."

"I can handle that."

"Good, then it's settled," Todd said while saluting.

The trio's first order of business was to decide that entering from the rear access through the kitchen would be less conspicuous.

"Whew! does something smell like shit or what?" Playlen asked. Another four-letter gem passed down by his teenaged-brother, Warren—Dink had inherited many more.

"Just the joint being closed u...," Todd said.

"No, it's got to be the genuine article; a dog or something must've wandered in here," Dink stated.

"Pretty smart pooch to get in here, huh?" Tim said.

"Look at the oven. The door is wide open; maybe someone burnt something in there and that's what stinks." The other two boys turned toward the cooking and baking appliance.

"You must be talking about those ghosts again, *huh*, Tim?" Todd pushed his brother playfully. "Nope, nothing in here."

Tim walked to the refrigerator, bent down, and picked up an object that was lying next to the cooling and freezing appliance. "An empty fresh-frozen orange juice can."

"Is it Minute Maid?" Todd asked as he took the can from Tim. "That's my favorite. Bing Crosby drinks it, too. Said so on a TV commercial the other night. He said, 'For PEP, for VITAL...it makes me feel younger'—or he said something like that."

"I've always wondered how anything can be considered fresh after it's been frozen," Tim said as he took the Minute Maid tin back from his twin.

"Write your congressman," Dink said grabbing the air- filled OJ container, "he'll tell you; politicians know everything except the answer to this riddle: What's brown and lies in the forest?" The citrus can hit the floor and rolled to a stop beside a red garbage container.

"We don't know."

"Winnie's pooh!"

"Real funny," Tim said with a slight chuckle. Let's get back to business."

"Hey, man, the Barrens didn't have a dog, did they?" Todd said.

"If they did, they must have kept it hidden," Tim said.

With Link in their thoughts, the three boys started their investigation to nose-out the awful odor.

Tim and Todd were heading up the twisting staircase to the second floor of the *new meeting house*? Dink was searching downstairs. He started in the living room...he noticed so many old blood stains that they seemed like part of the decor. "As long as there's no fresh ones added."

As he was crossing over the dull, red-and-white throw rug toward the fireplace, Dink noticed some dark spots where the bodies had obviously been found. He quickly turned away.

"This is creepy," he stated to nobody.

Dink noticed that a couch and love seat, both covered up with old sheets which were turning yellow, sat beside the throw rug. He looked under the cover that hid the chair-built-for-two. "Redwood—began its life as a Sequoia."

Dink walked bent over so that no one outside would notice him through the *Usher* windows. His investigation led him into the dining room, where rays from the sunset were flowing through the windowpanes into-and-out of an enormous chandelier, causing a dusty, purple-and-crimson maze of sunlight.

"I bet they never served 'potato turbate' in this fancy space."

Dink heard shuffling in the back area of the manor and ran in that direction. As he was closing in on the kitchen door, it suddenly flew open and hit him square in the nose. Link was standing on the other side. Link started moving very gently into the formal eating room; he was hurting from his swats. Now, his *double* was also in pain.

"How'd it go with Principal PegLeg?" Dink said, as he massaged his smeller.

"It was strange. Coffery will get his one day." Link Playlen held a fist toward the ceiling.

"What'ya me...?"

"Uh, maybe I'll tell you later. Anything start yet? What's that terrible smell?"

"No...no meeting yet. We've been trying to track down the stink. Tim and Todd are hunting upstairs."

At the top of the long, winding stairs, the Tender boys had split up, hoping to complete the probe in half the time. The gang's scheduled agenda was running behind.

Todd started looking in what must've been the master bedroom. "Not much in here, you locate anything yet?"

"No, not yet, huh."

Tim wandered into a sitting room at the end of a hallway that seemed to go on forever. There was a faded, navy blue-and-white carpet hiding the whole floor of the hall. Tim noticed that the few pieces of furniture left in the sitting room were protected by blotchy bedsheets.

"**Hey**! man, sure you haven't found anything?" Todd yelled, as he was leaving the master bedroom and making his way down the hall.

"No, but I can still smell it, whatever it is." Tim left the sitting room and entered the room across the hall; this chamber had probably been the young boy's because there were little toy nut-crackers and large toy soldiers scattered all around the place. He wandered into the closet, the door was open.

"**Hey**! there's a ladder in here nailed to the back wall of the closet."

Tim's twin walked in. "Climb up and see what's up there; it's probably an attic. Maybe somebody took a dump up there and that's what smells."

"Are you crazy? You go up."

"Sometimes, I think you are a sissy."

Todd went up the ladder quicker than a fireman trying to make a rescue. He came back down even faster, as if there was an actual blaze.

"There's a hole in the attic next to a tree with a piece of wood on the floor that looks like it was once used to cover the bare spot. Maybe Dink can tell us what kind of wood it is?" Todd rubbed his eyes.

"Sounds like a good escape route in case the cops show up unannounced."

It was no secret in town that the civic cops were amateurs. The state police had been summoned to crack the Barren mystery, but the pros had been too busy tracking a notorious outlaw named J. McCarthy and couldn't break free. Before the Barrens' tragedy, the biggest case in the community happened the time someone let the air out of the tires of the one-and-only squad car. The locals investigated that Capone-style caper for two months but never tracked down the *wisekids*.

"Here's the bathroom." Todd had a hard time pushing back the door. Tim followed him in.

"Man, the Barrens must not have used this room very often, not enough work on the door, probably why it stinks so bad in the joint," Todd said. "The stench is getting stronger." Todd inched toward the yellow porcelain bathtub. Tim stopped just inside the door.

Everything in the upstairs' restroom was an ugly, amber shade: the tub, the sink, the *crapper*, even the shower curtain, which had yellow daisies all over it.

Todd's nose sensed that this was where the awful smell was coming from; he hesitated, then yanked back the daisies. Tim looked away. He looked back. Tim was tingling inside; his emotions were stuck in the gray area between being scared and being excited.

Todd grabbed the flashlight-on-a-key-chain out of his dungarees and pointed it in the direction of the bathtub's bottom. He fixed the flash lamp on a body below. A bulk was blown up and nearly the same shade of blue as the navy blue uniform that covered it. Dried blood trailed from what remained of the right hand down to the drain. The face below the mouth was also coated with the crusty red stuff. Todd noticed the blue-and-yellow patch on the right sleeve: *Den 63*. Something made him look up.

"**Shiiiit!**" Todd screamed, turned, and rushed out of the room, almost knocking Tim on his rear end. Tim ran after his brother. The Tender boys were taught not to curse, but, at that moment, Todd could only utter one of Dink's favorite expressions.

Todd flew down the stairs, passed the Playlen twins, and headed directly for the back door. Tim, Link, and Dink finally caught him two blocks away from Chimera Road.

Todd was bent over; he was losing the lunch special he had consumed in the school cafeteria. Tim was smacking his twin's back, at the same time, keeping his tennis shoes away from the ground meat and onions mixed with mashed potatoes *waterfalling* from his brother's mouth.

"What's the ma...?" Tim asked. "What a mess." He turned away from the spew on the ground.

"Now that's a hell of a stink," Dink added, pinching his nose shut, "no doubt where that's coming from."

"Man, do...don't go back there, w...we gotta go home."

"That scream was a blood-wrencher," Link said, "it took the starch right out of my pants."

"Whata squeal," Dink said delicately.

"Link, how'd it go with PegLeg, huh?" Tim questioned.

"Weird, very weird."

Drops of sweat were starting to develop on Todd's forehead. He wiped his head and mouth with a sweater sleeve. "Ma...man you won't believe what's up in that bathroom and what I...I saw."

"Wait 'til I tell you guys what I saw in Coffery's office," Link returned. "Here, Todd, take some Beeman's."

"You first, Todd," Tim said.

"Ther...there's a dead body; it ha...had to be de... dead. No...no, it was definitely dead. The face was awf..."

"Stay cool," Link said.

"What was it?" the remaining officers of the Tender/ Playlen Club said in unison.

"It wa...was a body dressed in a cub scout uniform. Then, boom! a fa...fat guy dressed in a cook's outfit appeared. He was holding a huge kn...knife and pointing it at the kid. That's when I bolted."

Link temporarily forgot about the pain in his butt. "It's the same thing I saw at PegLeg's window. It really scared me but then I thought I was just seeing things— Coffery smacked me good."

"What are you carrying on about?" his brother said.

"Each time Coffery would whack me, I would see more of what Todd just thought he saw. I couldn't see its face, though."

"No, I didn't see the face, either."

"Look, we have to go back up there and see who's in the tub," Tim pleaded, thinking that he could never enjoy *submarines* in that bathtub. "Then we have to call the law. It's the right thing to do, huh?" Tim Tender thought that they should investigate the situation, even though he knew if he saw the dead body, it would probably give him bad dreams for a week.

"Are you nuts? I'm not going anywhere near that place, ever again," Todd said with conviction.

"Are you full of it, Tim?" Dink said. "What if they blame us for that dead kid? Besides, I don't think the cops would like us being in there."

"Man, they wouldn't charge us with anything, would they?" the president said.

"Dink's cool; we can't let anyone know we've been in the joint," the vice president remarked.

In the next moment, Todd's portable electric light went out—the Burgess batteries had gone dead.

The items scheduled to be discussed at the gang's gathering were reduced to a single topic—they didn't even bother calling the meeting to order.

Tim spoke: "What do we do about the body in the tub?"

Todd raised his right arm. "Let's vote."

It was a three-to-one decision that they would all go home after ringing the police about the cub scout. The identification of the caller would be a fake name.

Each T&P member pedaled like never before, periodically checking over his shoulder to see that nothing ghostly was following him.

Chapter 2

The day that the cub scout had been found dead started out pretty routine: *slow,* the way most people preferred it.

"Mom gave us a lot of clothes to hang up this morning," Todd said.

"Last weekend of summer always brings a bunch of dirty duds from jamming all the playing duties into the final days," Tim explained, as he lowered his teaspoon into a bright blue bowl full of Rice Crispies and doused with strawberry Kool-Aid.

"How can you eat cereal without milk?" Todd asked. He pushed a tablespoon into a bigger blue bowl overflowing with shredded wheat and Elsie's.

"You know I can't stand that white stuff; besides, Kool-Aid seems to make the *snap, crackle, and pop* last longer. I'm charmed by the sound."

"And, I think you caused the mutt to run away, putting that stuff on his Wheaties. Mrs. Jasper said she saw Frisky heading up the street chasing a milk truck."

"Then he never came back. I know. I may have misjudged his tail-wagging at my refreshment choice."

"Don't blame yourself; I was just kidding. That mutt was always getting out and running somewhere. The last time he just couldn't find his way back. I guess we should've had a taller fence."

"But, I miss him almost as much as Grandpa and Grandma."

"Me too."

The twins' grandfather had died almost a year earlier from Leukemia, caused by, according to Dad Tender, the Lucky Strikes he seemed to be smoking constantly.

Grandmother Tender was never the same after that and died a short time later. Tim and Todd had loved spending weekends at their grandparents' home on Auburn Street.

"Come on, we've got to go make the beds and then head for school," Todd told his younger twin as he pushed open the swinging door that led into the dining room.

"Yuck, Mrs. Long's class; I hate that speech she makes her new students give about their summer vacation," Tim uttered, following Todd down the hall toward their bedroom, one of four.

"I know, I know. You don't like to talk in front of anyone unless you know them like a brother. It's really no big deal."

"My stomach is starting to feel like I just ate a whole box of Good 'N' Plenties after watching Vincent Price in *House of Wax*."

Todd stood up, Tim stood up next to him—Todd was a couple inches shorter, blond, wide-shouldered, looked like a muscular bagel. He had a strong face that could probably take a punch from "The Champ," Rocky Marciano, and not even flinch. Tim had beaten a respiratory disease when he was a baby and was slim. He was dark-haired and reminded people of a tall pretzel. He had a slender face reminiscent, he claimed comically, of some characters in the movie about a traitor in a Nazi POW camp, *Stalag 17*.

They were both dressed in bootless, John Wayne-type outfits: plaid cowboy shirts; stiff black pants folded up from the bottom; and Keds tennis shoes.

"You know, your bed doesn't even look like you slept in it. How do you do that?"

"I just like to be neat," Tim said, as he hung up a striped garment in his closet, where all his shirts were spaced exactly an inch apart with all the top buttons buttoned. His pants were all draped over hangers with the leg bottoms stretching down the exact length as the waist tops, touching like Siamese twins. As he left the room, he blew a taunting kiss to his brother and patted his images on the plaster of Karloff, Lorre, and March. "I'll meet you outside, better shake a leg."

Todd was struggling: "Man, I can't ever seem to get these covers straight. How does he do that?" He settled for mitts, baseballs, and bats folded over identical mitts, baseballs, and bats. "Good enough. Mom'll fix it."

"Come on, Todd, we've got to meet the Playlens before school starts," Tim said hurriedly, as he pushed Todd's Schwinn *Traveler* toward him opening a *louie* grip. Todd grabbed the bike *rightie*.

They pedaled furiously down Twenty-fifth Street in the direction of sixth grade.

Chapter 3

"You guys ready for Mrs. Long, huh?" Tim said. "She isn't nearly as great as Miss Tester; I've heard stories about her no-messing-around approach to teaching. I don't know if I can handle that stupid vacation speech, huh?"

"Don't worry, it'll be cool," Link said, "besides, you and Todd ought to have that summertime sermon down pat by now, considering you Tenders go to the same place every year."

Dink, dressed in bluejeans, white T-shirt—sleeves rolled up, had a pinky finger in one of his ears; he was always trying to clean the wax out of his drums. Dink had this thing about wax: he felt that any excess buildup left alone might cause him to go deaf; hence, the digit dance.

The boys planted their Keds—Tim's and Todd's, white with black labels; Link's, red with red insignias and shoelaces to match his red beanie, red T, and red jeans; and Dink's, black with white emblems—in the dirt next to the oleander bush in front of Mrs. Grumbel's four-room, white-and-red shack. She was Head Custodian at Lakeside and lived on the grounds.

"Okay, let's bring the meeting to order. All for Todd being President of the T&P club, raise your right hand," Todd said with confidence.

Four right arms extended toward the cloudless blue sky, and the motion collected a *second* three times.

"Do I also hear a second on President Tender deciding the offices that the remaining members will hold during our final year of elementary school?"

"I second," Tim Tender said.

"Good. Then it's settled."

"What about reelections, Mr. President?" Dink asked.

"Four-year terms, good until the end of junior high."

"Mr. President! What about a place for our clubhouse?" Link asked. He rubbed his palms and licked his lips as if staring at a T-bone steak.

"After the final bell, we're going to check out the abandoned mansion on Chimera Road."

"**The old Barren place**! Are you nuts, huh? Sorry, I didn't mean to yell," Tim said as he put his hands over his mouth.

"It's perfect," Dink said, "nobody goes near the place anymore."

"That's because the Barrens were all massacred there," Tim said, "how 'bout we build a tree house?"

"Let's vote," the president said. All for a house in a tree like everybody else has, raise your right hand."

Only one set of five fingers went up: Tim's.

"Now, all those for the Barrens', raise your right hand."

Three went up.

"Good. Then it's settled. Next meeting starts promptly at four-forty-four this afternoon."

Link took off his red beanie and placed it over one corner of the "Beware of the Killer Hound" sign, which was next to the one that stated, "No Trespassing." The small billboards were in the middle of Mrs. Grumbel's yard, a lawn that was perfect, during a Sunshine State rainstorm, for mud football.

"Do you think if we stand here long enough the old crank will come out?" Link wondered.

"I hope so; I love seeing her get riled up," Todd responded.

"Yea, when she starts getting that gimpy leg going, it's a riot," Dink added as he started limping like Long John Silver, "reminds me of PegLeg."

"We shouldn't be in her yard," Tim said; "besides, we gotta get moving, the bell will ring any minute, huh?"

Suddenly, old lady Grumbel threw open her dusty screen door and started screaming at them to get away from her house. Of course, no sounds came out of her mouth. She waddled down the flimsy wooden stairs, pulling up paint chips with her steel-toed boots. According to Mrs. Grumbel, she wasn't able to move like she used to because of the oversized veins that had developed on her left leg. When she was after one of them, most of the Lakeside kids felt different about the tempo of her gait. Tim used to think that one of Mrs. Grumbel's arms was longer than the other but later realized that it was only the Miller High Life beer she usually held in her hand.

The kids rushed around to the front of the schoolhouse before Grumbel could catch them. The four boys ran up the stairs and into the north entrance. Without hesitation, they escaped into the bathroom—or so they thought. After stopping sharply against the hard, shiny white urinals, three boys searched around the room. Somebody was missing—it was Link. The remaining trio immediately raced out of the restroom, then screamed and stared right into Grumbel's boil-covered face. She had the back of Link's neck in her giant hand—the crippled hand. On that grip, her right, she had lost her thumb and forefinger, while the other three fingers had been burnt together in a one-car Chevy crash. The collision that Mr. Grumbel had died in. He had been the Head Chef at Lakeside Elementary.

The director of Klara's Funeral Parlor, A. Hister—a short and smallish man—had had a colossal casket made to fit Mr. G's 365-pound corpse. The only parts of his body that weren't buried with him were his left forearm, wrist, and hand; they had been missing from the area around the smashup and were never located.

"Let go of Link, you witch," Dink commanded while backing away from the large custodian.

"Yea, man, he didn't do anything." Todd also retreated and stepped on his brother's feet.

"Ow! huh, Todd?" Tim gave his brother a shove.

Mrs. Grumbel whipped out the paper pad that she carried like a pistol in a leather holster strapped to her left leg. After the accident, she had become very nasty and stopped talking and started drinking. The auto tragedy had taken place over three years ago, about the time of the Barren bloodbath. She had always claimed that they had been run off the road by a black hot rod with dark windows and flames on the fenders. The cops never located such a vehicle.

Grumbel wrote: *You boys better scram or end up in the principal's office like your little friend here. If I could run you down, you'd all suffer the consequences of Coffery's wrath.* She then began to push Link down the hall.

"**Be tough, Link,**" his sibling yelled. The Playlens were sturdy kids like Todd Tender; they were all built better for physical pain than Tim. Although, Timothy was weight training to try and build himself a solid, wiry frame. The Playlens' parents had always said that they were rearing small versions of Ernest Borgnine: wide faces, strong jaws, and dark hair. And, even though the Playlen kids' mugs were only eleven-years old, they had to be shaved once-a-week. The four twin buddies were precocious to say the least but had many friends with all levels of abilities.

"**Hang in there, Link, man,**" Todd screamed, as his pal and Mrs. Grumbel got farther down the corridor.

"**Link, don't let PegLeg get the better of you,**" Tim added.

Tim felt terrible...he knew first hand what Link was in for....In 1953 Tender had experienced the principal's wrath for something he didn't even do. He got caught and the real outlaw escaped. Tim Tender wasn't a "fink," and it cost him dearly.

The incident happened in the south restroom on the first floor. That day, Tim had to do a number "two" in the worst way and was excused from Miss Tester's room, his fifth-grade teacher at the time. While he was doing his business on one of the cleanest toilets in the county—thanks to Mrs. Grumbel—and staring at his reflection in the polished chrome latch, Tim heard Tinkle Jones—a sixth grader...a big one—come in, talking to himself. Tim said that Tinkle repeated over and over, "I'll show that witch." After cleaning his function at hand, Tim opened the stall door and immediately noticed a yellow puddle on the previously spotless floor. He moved directly to make a speedy exit—Tim didn't even stop to wash his hands, a minor miracle. But, luck wasn't on his side, he bumped into a gigantic body. The huge frame was possessed by Mrs. Grumbel.

The next thing that Tim found himself doing was assuming the position and bracing himself on Coffery's maple desk.

Rod, Tim and Todd's older brother, had already advised his younger siblings about a strategy to use against the "Welt Warrior." Coffery's scheme was to pound away until the kid started sobbing—out of control. Big brother said that if Todd or Tim was ever nailed by PegLeg, acting like a wimp and not a hero would save some of the suffering.

Not to be too obvious, Tim started crying after his third stinging swat, and Principal PegLeg stopped. Tim was thankful...one more pelt and shamming would never have entered the scene.

Before Deacon Coffery had arrived in St. Petersburg and became principal, a job for which it had been difficult to find willing candidates, he ran a Texaco that was attached to a motel on *Route 66* in Arizona. His resume also stated that he had worked part-time in a doctor's office.

And preceding the gas-station stint—according to him—he had been honorably discharged from the Army as a Lieutenant Colonel. He told the townsfolk that he had lost his leg in *W.W.II*, for which he received a Purple Heart....He also claimed to have the Silver Star for single-handedly killing four Nazi soldiers. No one in town had ever seen either medal, or ever asked about them.

Chapter 4

PegLeg Coffery was mean, simple as that.

Link Playlen started to sweat.

One trick Coffery used was to make a kid wait—and wait some more. Then, his scheme was to pound away until his victim starting sobbing—out of control. He kept notches on the "flogger," representing each kid that came out of his office with red, watery eyes. PegLeg had made the "swatter" himself in the Industrial Arts classroom, so that all his potential customers could see what they had coming if they dared cross him. Principal Coffery raised suffering to a lofty level...it was as if he was an artist and the "holy paddle" was his brush.

Link was squirming in a honey maple seat. It was afternoon, and with his morning visit, the second time his rear end had agonized in the chair located in the office just outside Coffery's internal sanctum.

"Hey, can't you tell him I'm in a hurry?"

"Not me." Eve Brown, the principal's secretary, was chewing and popping her Wrigley's. **Pop! Pop! Pop!**—*Chinese Water Torture*, like Link saw used in the war movies at the Park Theater, the neighborhood cinema house, would have been easier to take. She also wore, as on most days, a school- week's worth of perfume—Link guessed Chanel No. 5—and it was beginning to burn his eyes and make him queasy.

"You ever think about cuttin' back on the smelly stuff?"

"Deacon likes my essence. So, shut up."

"Oh, now you're calling him Deacon. Cozy."

"Uh...uh, I mean Mr. Cof...Coffery."

Link shifted his head and stared passed the assistant's puffy, strawberry-blonde hairdo at the black nameplate with red lettering on Coffery's amber-colored door. PegLeg had a thing for honey maple—even the area where his leg was missing below the knee was made of the yellow-finished wood, with a gold-plated cover embracing the portion that touched the floor. Every kid in Lakeside knew when Coffery was coming for him, or her. There was even an allegation, never proven, that he once kicked a kid with his wooden body part. After that incident, the older students had tagged their principal with the nickname, "PegLeg."

Link's pale blue peepers were fixed on the nameplate: "Principal Deacon Coffery."

The secretary spoke and broke Link out of his trance: "You're not scared, are you?" She had a shrill voice unlike any other in the small community.

"Me, nah, I'm cool," Link responded, trying to hide his real feelings. He was plenty scared, but he was acting tough.

"I don't know; I've seen Deacon bring a kid to his knees with just one swat," Eve said.

"I don't sweat PegLeg." Link's shifting continued unwittingly.

"Could've fooled me."

Suddenly, the moniker on the door began to disappear from Link's view, and a six-foot-three-inch body filled the empty space. Link's eyeballs immediately focused on the scar that began just below Coffery's right eye; continued up and over the bridge of his nose; curved down; and ended below his left jaw. Just as quickly, Link's vision turned to PegLeg's dark, greasy, extra-heavy hair. Playlen couldn't imagine Audrey Hepburn running her fingers through that oily mane. Deacon's black eyes—strangely, there was very little white part—were wide open, as if he was getting an uncommon pleasure from Link's predicament.

"Young master Playlen, how are you today?" the principal said.

"I'm cool; let's get this over with." He sprung up as if bouncing off a trampoline.

"What's the rush? Get what over with? What is it that you think that I'm going to do to you?"

"The same thing you do to every kid."

"Possibly you're correct. I have someone in here that wants to meet you." At that moment, the maple slammed shut.

"Isn't Miss Brown going to witness?" Link asked. He pointed at the back of the door.

"No need."

"I'm assuming the position; let's go, I've got a meeting to attend." He stared down at Coffery's desk and readied himself for pain.

Coffery took the padlock off the file cabinet top drawer, pulled out a thick book, placed it on a table, picked up the discipline weapon, and put the text back quickly. "Mr. Playlen, I would like to introduce *Alois*, named after my mentor's father." Every Lakeside kid with an older brother was already familiar with the term. A few younger sisters knew it, too.

"Yea, fine, let's move along here," Link pleaded. He just wanted to get out of there. He eyeballed all the nicks on the "bashing board."

"Just let me take a couple of practice swings. I don't want to pull a muscle and hurt myself...this time is going to be special."

"The only muscle you have is in your head."

"What did you say? I didn't understand you."

"Nothing. Nothing."

It was at the conclusion of the *first* biting blow that Link got his initial glimpse of the ghost. He thought that he saw a hat like the ones the cooks wore on the serving line at the Webb's City Cafeteria.

Blam! For the *second* time *Alois* met Link's posterior with a passion. "What the dev...?" Playlen whispered as an enormous body appeared wearing salt-and-pepper pants and a stained uniform shirt. The sighting seemed to be floating next to the window.

"Are you ready to say 'Uncle' yet?" Coffery said.

Blam! **Blam**! *Three* and *Four* made their mark. Deacon was getting impatient...the kid was stronger than he had anticipated.

"If you think you're going to defeat me, think again," Coffery said.

Link could barely think at all, and then, **Blam**! number *five* came alive. Playlen then thought he saw a long butcher knife, with blade sparkling, held by the same scary specter. Was he in a trance from the unbearable pain? Link began to cry.

"Ha, you'll never conquer the king," the principal said in triumph.

When Link Playlen was finally released from the torture chamber, he felt something warm on his right hand. It was a bit of blood trickling down toward his fingers. There was a small slice in the tender part of his hand between the thumb and forefinger. He pulled out a *Spanky* handkerchief from his red jeans' pocket and wiped off the blood.

Apparently, Coffery hadn't seen the silent poltergeist that Link thought he had encountered—PegLeg was having too much fun. Link didn't mention it for fear of possibly ending up at St. Sid's Sanitorium.

It was four-forty, and Link was late as he ran against time; he only had four minutes to get to the Barren clubhouse.

Chapter 5

About an hour after darkness had settled over St. Petersburg on the horrifying Monday that the cub scout was discovered dead, Tim and Todd edged their way into the front door of their lavender-colored home.

"You realize it's past curfew time," Tim stated as he started to tiptoe.

"I know, man; the third degree is going to start without delay. Watch and see. There's no sense in tiptoeing."

The elder twin was right.

Within ten minutes of the hardball questioning, Todd blurted out the episode about the cub scout but not the specter. Neither Tender twin mentioned anything about the other set of twins that had been present at the already-defunct clubhouse.

Mom Tender, Dad Tender, and their Tender sons piled into the family Ford demonstrator—Father Tender was a top-notch car salesman at Grant Ford, downtown on Ninth Street, one of the main avenues for buildings of business.

The family motored toward the local "yokel" cop shop.

* * *

"That's okay, Mr. Tender, we've already received a tip from a Mr. Seymour Butz and are already on the case," the sheriff said.

"That's right," the deputy added, "I recognized the deceased boy; his family moved to Palmetto," as he pointed in a southerly direction, "a couple of years back."

"Who was he?" Tim asked. "What about the blood?"

"You can get to Palmetto now by way of the new bridge, the Sunshine Skyway," Todd added, "it's really high at the top." His hand was above his head.

"Just don't go jumping off." The sheriff made a motion as if diving off the high dive at the Spa Pool, the inside pool located downtown near the Million Dollar Pier.

"Eddie Liebowitz," the under-sheriff mentioned, "we're waiting on the autopsy report, but we think he drowned. His right thumb and forefinger and half his tongue were sliced off and are missing."

"Look," the sheriff was getting impatient, "we've got things under control; so, you Tenders can be on your Tender way."

"That's clever, John," the deputy remarked, as he encircled his arms around the family and moved them out the door.

"Thanks, Jack. You all have a nice evening."

* * *

While sitting in the back seat of the car, Tim and Todd knew that discipline would be the next item on their parents' program.

"Man, what do you think they're going to do this time?" Todd asked. "It'll be the second time you've been punished today. Are you trying to set a record?" His mouth was inches away from his brother's right ear.

"I can't believe Mrs. Long made me sit in the closet just because I refused to do that stupid vacation report.

It's dark in there, huh."

"You're just going to have to do it tomorrow or make a trip to Coffery's office?"

Tim ignored that remark. "You know Todd, there's no way the Liebowitz kid could've been drowned at the Barrens'; the pipes there have been dried up for years."

"Why would someone take the time to bring him to that death house? I can't believe I wanted to make that place a clubhouse." He swiped his forehead as if relieved by the gesture.

"It's got to be haunted. My question is why would a ghost want to kill an innocent kid and then cut off his fingers and tongue and go to the trouble of removing them but not the body, huh?"

"Had to be the same ghost that I saw there and Link kept seeing in Coffery's office, don't you think? Carrying that big knife."

"How could anybody kill a cub scout, it's un-American, ghost or no ghost."

"What are you boys whispering about back there?"

"Nothing Mom!" The twins spoke together. They had never been exposed to anything like the mysterious experience at the Barrens' mausoleum and were, for now, keeping their reputations as sane individuals. *Possibly*, awaiting further proof.

"Okay," Dad Tender said, "we'll give you a choice of whom you want to hand out the reprimands."

Father Tender worked long hours at his job and, also, during the summer, helped coach Todd and Tim's little league baseball team. He didn't have time for creative chastisement; therefore, he would just ground the kids for so long they began to feel like bears in hibernation. The kids disliked that form of corrective measure the most. And, when given the right to choose, they usually opted for the female spouse in the Mr. & Mrs. Tender partnership. Her versions were more swift, all of which, as well as their dad's, were justified. No indiscriminate punishments.

"Mom can hand down the decision," the boys said, "how 'bout going to bed without our supper?" The boys knew that the menu on Monday nights was always "liver 'n' onions," and they could pass on that meal anytime. If they could pull this coup off, Todd's and Tim's stomachs would thank them for days. The problem was that though their parents were lenient in granting the choice of temporary warden, the type of discipline was never bartered.

"Sorry," Mother Tender said as she turned her head around to face her children, "come home directly after school for the next two weeks, no seeing your friends or passing *Go*. Her left pinky was wagging and making its way into the rear portion of the Ford.

"Oh, Ma, come on." She had hoodwinked her twin sons, and their hope of a speedy penalty never materialized.

"Your mother has spoken," Dad Tender said, as he momentarily took one hand off the steering wheel and pulled his left thumb and forefinger across his mouth as if to close a zipper.

Chapter 6

The Tender twins finally got their *get-out-of-jail-free card* on the Friday following the Friday that ended the first five days of the new educational year. They were due to spend the evening at the Playlens' abode.

Things had quieted down in the small town since the poor cub scout had advanced to "the great explorer den in the Heavens." The Liebowitz kid had been missing from his home in Palmetto for a couple of weeks. The coroner's report confirmed drowning as the cause of death. The St. Petersburg cops said that they didn't have a clue or a lead, which came as no surprise to the citizens of the community.

"Do you think Dink and Link's mom and dad will be themselves tonight?" Tim asked his brother.

"Friday night, the start of the weekend; I doubt it."

Tim and Todd arrived at the Playlen home late afternoon. The Tenders walked side by side up the pink steps, each grasping a pink railing, and together knocked Tender knocks on the pink front door of the pink house.

"Sloppy Joes and French fries tonight." Todd licked his lips with his tongue.

"Great bill of fare; I'm excited," Tim added.

The T&P gang always looked forward to Friday darkness.

Mrs. Playlen answered the door as *Christine*. Mr. Playlen, a few inches shorter than his wife, stepped out from behind her dressed as *Claude*. Her given name was Golda, his Erik, but both designations went down the river during these bizarre episodes.

They would occasionally act out, in full wardrobe, scenes from their favorite movie, *The Phantom of the Opera*, and remain that way for days.

Christine turned to her husband and said: "Oh, *Claude*, you are the Phantom!" She swirled around as if on air, "How are you boys doing tonight?"

"Just fine, how about yourselves?" Tim said. He turned and whispered to his brother. "They're at it again."

"The guys are in their bedroom; go on back," *Claude* said.

The Tenders walked through the living room; continued to the dining room, which was beside *Christine* and *Claude's* bedroom; through the swinging door; passed the butcher-block table in the middle of the kitchen; and into Link and Dink's inner sanctuary.

Link and Dink's bedroom contained a large window that faced the Cemetery Hill Graveyard, where Mr. Grumbel had been *laid to rest*. The back of his headstone was in full view.

On the walls of the room, there were posters of the Our Gang Kids and the Three Stooges-plus-one—Shemp, the fourth Stooge, who really wasn't.

Todd stared at the Stooges' banners: "Hey, Dink, I've always meant to ask you, why don't they call Larry, 'Curly' Larry, and Joe, who's mostly bald, plain old Joe?"

"You got me. Must be in the script the other way."

"Remember the time Dad and Mom wanted to save some *moola* and gave us both 'bowl' cuts and made us look like Moe. Not cool," Link added.

"Man, that was a riot," Todd said.

"Let's go eat." Dink pointed toward the door, and the foursome was off to the dining room for dinner at the Playlen Opera House Cafe.

"I can't believe I ate two Joes and two helpings of fries; I'm stuffed to the gills and back," Tim said, rubbing his belly. "They were great, huh?"

"I had three and could've had another," Todd said. "What'd your mom do to them tonight; they were especially good, man." He kissed his fingers like an Italian chef.

"She's started putting some mystery ingredient in them and won't reveal the secret," Link said as he sat down on the bottom half of the stacked beds.

"Yea, not even to Dad," Link's sibling added.

After dinner, the boys had been treated to an act from the Playlen rendition of *The Phantom* and then sent off to fantasyland to be followed by dreamland.

The gang was allowed to watch one movie before hitting the sleeping bags. The Playlen twins had the television box, a brand new Westinghouse "Capri" model that swiveled for easy viewing in any direction, in their room.

"Hey, guys, how come your parents allow you to have the TV in here?" Todd questioned.

"Dink answered: "Because the living room's too formal, and they have way too many movie props in the master bedroom."

"And nobody can be in Warren's room for too long," Link said.

"You mean Stinky's pad, don't you?" Todd said.

"It's the old socks that he never washes," Dink said, "once he hit a home run in gym class with dirty socks on— he's superstitious now."

After calling the meeting to order; reading the previous gathering's minutes; discussing finances; and dispensing of old business, it was time for the boys to make a decision on which horror flick to inhale the life out of that night—an overcast, muggy night.

"Okay," Todd said, "there are three movies being broadcast tonight—each at the same time on different channels. Mr. Secretary/Treasurer, please list them and explain the rules for voting."

"Yes, sir, Mr. President," Tim said. "The choices are *Frankenstein*, *Mad Love*, and *Dr. Jekyll and Mr. Hyde*. Each member should write on a secret ballot one, two, or three in your order of preference. The flick with the lowest total will win the vote."

Tim wanted to watch *Mad Love* because he loved Peter Lorre and his evil-looking eyes. Tim Tender thought that "Pop-eyes" played the part of the obsessed Dr. Gogol with delicious reality. Peter Lorre and Boris Karloff were Tim's favorite actors—*Frankenstein* was his second choice.

Tim, part of his duties being secretarial, tallied the papers. "Okay, the poll plays out like this: *Frankenstein* scores nine, *Mad Love,* eight, and *Dr. Jekyll and Mr. Hyde*, seven. Movie three wins numbers down."

"Great. Turn on the tube and let's get watching, man," Todd said as he got comfortable in one of the four lawn chairs brought in for that evening. Link got up from the bed and flipped on the television dial. Then, the triad not already seated found their places. The T&P gang loved to be scared by motion pictures, so any pick would have been fine. The frightening film did its job superbly, and all the boys were fast asleep shortly after the finale. The Playlen kids had bunkbeds but wanted to snooze alongside the Tenders. The folding chairs were put away and replaced by four sleeping bags. They all slumbered in a perfect line, at least they started out that way.

Tim Tender's breadbasket was rebelling against the extra sandwich when he heard a disturbing clamor outside the big windowpane. He didn't stand up, he didn't jump up, he raised up, as if someone or something was pulling him. He started to float in midair in the area of the huge glass. Tim was staring down at Todd, Link, Dink, and another Tim? They were as still as freshly-embalmed corpses.

"What in Heaven's name is going on here?"

Each kid had a granite headstone, with streaks of dark fungus gripping each, above his head.

"There's writing on the tombstones." Tim focused his eyes but couldn't make out any letters. "Todd...Dink... Li...wake up, help me!" They didn't seem to hear him.

Tim glided through the bedroom window and noticed an oak branch on the ground below that had been disjointed from its home tree. The piercing wind in the *boneyard* pushed the fog from cemetery headstone to cemetery headstone. It was time for the thick mist to leave its present tombstone and advance to a new address of the dead.

Tim Tender was now moving in a kind of limbo over the graveyard.

"There's so many burial plots. They look like sardines stuffed into a can. There must be millions of graves."

Suddenly it began to rain, a shower so severe that it didn't hit the soil in a straight line.

"Great! Now it's raining cats and dogs; this can't be a dream."

Tim's second (first?) body began to levitate and move back toward the window and eventually crashed down on Chef Grumbel's resting place. Tim wiped his eyes and read the testimonial written on Mr. Grumbel's burial marker:

"Fat you may have been, my heart loved you as if your body was thin. Glinda Grumbel, your loving wife. Nice sentiment.*"*

Suddenly, the earth beneath his feet began to *shake, rattle, and roll*. He was being raised up again—a huge pinewood coffin broke through the former dry dirt as if Mother Earth was spitting out a polluted piece of land. It lifted Tim Tender up and up and up until he finally fell off, down to the muddy landscape of Cemetery Hill. For a brief moment, Tim was reminded of the story, *Moby Dick*, that he had read in one of Miss Tester's Literature lessons.

"Somebody help me! What kind of nightmare is this?"

Not a soul seemed to hear him.

Suddenly, Tim encountered an image: a rusty-colored dog ran down from the top of the steep hill. Tim blinked his eyes, then yelled, "**Frisky, Frisky**." But, the mutt quickly vanished. Tim did notice that the pooch's whiskers seemed to have some sort of white stuff on them.

In another second, a vision of his grandparents, arm-in-arm and laughing, appeared on the landscape but departed as sharply as his dog. "Grandma! Grandpa! Where are your going? Come back, I miss you." For a moment, Tim felt happy that they seemed happy. But, for a different moment, he was sad about Frisky.

Then! a final phantom, he hoped, showed on the scene— "it" rose up out of Mr. Grumbel's boggy chasm. The new sighting was wrapped by a colossal cook's uniform. The ghost was clutching a long butcher knife, blade glistening, pointing it at the pine coffin. Tim stared at one of the most shocking things of his *young* life. He turned away but was forced to look back.

"No way! A cub scout's blue-and-yellow scarf?" He wiped the rain from his eyes and hoped it was just an hallucination. A second glance. "Alright! It's gone."

Tim Tender then fixed his gaze on the specter, who was smiling a giant smile. He recognized the facial expression.

"**Mr. Grumbel, Mr. Grumbel**, what's going on? Did you kill Eddie Liebowitz?" Now, for some reason, Tim didn't seem afraid.

The ghost aimed the big pearl-handled dagger in the direction of the Playlen boys' bedroom and disappeared.

Fear returned instantly, and Tim was again floating over the four peaceful-looking bodies. He was being pushed towards the T&P members. He could *now* read the inscriptions on the markers that were entrenched above the officers' heads:

Todd Tender —	Born:	May 09, 1943	Died:	November 2, 1954
Link Playlen —	Born:	June 20, 1943	Died:	November 2, 1954
Dink Playlen —	Born:	June 20, 1943	Died:	November 2, 1954
Tim Tender —	Born:	May 09, 1943	Died:	November 2, 1954

The Sun's rays broke through the windowpane and into Tim's eyes, ending the bad dream. "It was just a nightmare, right? Maybe

I shouldn't have eaten the extra sandwich." He studied the bedroom, his buddies were gone, sleeping bags and all. Tim put his hands to his face and sweat was transferred from face to hands. He thought that he must have been perspiring a bunch because his *pjs* were soaked.

Tim didn't leave the inside of his snoring suitcase for a long period; he was too terrified. "Did I just see the ghosts of my missing mutt, my grandparents, and Head Chef Grumbel?"

Young Tender eventually stood up and walked toward the glass. "Nothing seems differ...wai...wait a minute. Tha...that huge rectangular hole in the cemetery wasn't there yesterday when Todd and I arrived." Then, it dawned on him that there was no one in the room to hear his statement of disbelief; he stopped talking.

Timothy went back to his sleeping bag and started rolling it up. In the process, a blue-and-yellow scarf fell to the floor.

Chapter 7

"Dink, where are you going so early? School doesn't start for another hour and a half."

Dink opened the rosy-colored door and passed through to the other side: "Lorraine's going to be at the library and I want to see her. Besides, we're going to decide our costumes for Halloween." He jumped on his blue Schwinn.

"Halloween's still two weeks away. I wouldn't be so serious about her if I were you. What do you know about her? She's only been here a little over a year."

"I know I like her and I think she likes me; I don't think PegLeg has a clue."

Miss Coffery had moved to Saint Petersburg from New York City, where she had been living with her mother, the former Mrs. Coffery. Lorraine's parents had met in Europe before the war ended and moved to Arizona—they divorced six years ago. Lorraine's mother escaped with her daughter from the Southwest and hightailed it to NYC in the Northeast and became a high-priced model, a career she continued until she died from malnutrition. She never ate anything. Lorraine had been forced to move to St. Petersburg and live with Principal Coffery.

"You know, Dink, Lorraine was a child model in the Big Apple."

"I know, she reminds me of Grace Kelly. Her looks are irresistible. See you later, Link."

"Watch yourself with her."

"What the devil does he mean by that?"

* * *

As Dink was nearing Lakeside, he saw many brownish-black birds circling and diving overhead like *W.W.II* fighter planes engaged in a dark-sky battle. They were buzzing around the burning lights that surrounded the tennis courts.

"What the crap are vultures doing here?"

Not really understanding why, Dink ran passed the brick schoolhouse; passed the asphalt kickball court; and down the small hill that approached the grass-and-dirt section of the playground. Out of the corner of his eye he saw some movement; he spun sharply to the left. "What's PegLeg doing out here?" Principal Coffery was just entering the delivery door of the school cafeteria. Dink continued to rotate a complete half-turn, a twirl executed with perfect precision—a move even the most accomplished Prima Ballerina would be proud to have in her repertoire. At the end of the twist, his eyes focused on a porch light. Underneath the electric glare, Mrs. Grumbel was awkwardly climbing up the steps of her shanty.

"She's out here, too?"

All of a sudden, the grim-looking birds landed everywhere on the recess grounds: the wooden gazebo, the wooden swing set, the wooden fence that encircled the tennis courts.

"What do you scavengers want? Waiting for something to die? Or is it already dead?"

Dink cautiously advanced on the row of tall palm trees that protected Lake Maggiore. The trunks and fronds of the palms stood firmly between Lakeside's recreation area and the chainlink barrier that enclosed the huge body of water, home to the powerful jaws and sharp teeth of many alligators.

The intimidating vultures—with plumage spread, heads bald, and beaks razor sharp—fell in line behind Dink, as if they were waiting for some military officer to roar out a marching cadence.

Dink immediately turned around: "Look, you creeps better quit following me, I'm not dead." Playlen did observe that the lead buzzard's right wing was deformed. "Probably a clash with one of his foul friends over road-kill cuisine."

Dink was being drawn to the watery home of Big Alvin and his reptile relatives. Big Alvin was the ten-foot alligator that had avoided becoming some rich socialite's purse or wallet for as many years as the Tender and Playlen twins had been alive. Everybody in town knew Big Alvin because a Swiss Army Knife had been gored into his hide by a drifter wearing a *NY Yankee* ball cap in a struggle that Alvin won. The blade remained stuck in the gator's backside just below his massive head.

Dink reminisced about the reptile-versus-man fight. "I wonder if that guy tasted like chicken to Big Alvin?" He chuckled slightly but the humor in the situation quickly faded.

When Dink finally reached the point where dry land became wet land, he performed an additional 180-degree pirouette, and the parading vermin stopped, bumping into each other like a chain-reaction car crash. The vultures fled the arena...they waited near by.

"I think I need to continue this search around the banks to the southwest. How do I know these things? Great, now I'm starting to sweat. I'm sure Lorraine will be impressed with underarm stains."

The Sun was rising in the East and beginning to filter through the towering palms making Dink's trek a little easier.

He halted, as if he had smashed into an invisible wall.

"O...oh, bo...boy! Wh...what's that?"

There was an object hovering about five feet above the fresh-water lake.

"That's not a vulture. Dink did a double-take; the sighting had sunlight streaming right through it. "It has to be the ghost that Link and Todd described. And it's got a big knife and pointing it downward."

Then, Dink discovered the purpose of his involuntary journey: a husky body floating face down in Lake Maggiore.

"Oh! damn! I don't think whatever that is is bobbing for apples."

The day's awakening was now complete. Dink saw that the water close to the body was darker than the rest of the lake. "That's got to be blood. But, what's the oily stuff near the head?" The head seemed to be drifting back and forth like a Pez with its top open, where some kid had tried to get the candy out. "Oh, shit! the neck is slit."

Suddenly, the oversized spook lunged forward; moved freely into-and-out of Dink's body; and vanished. Dink Playlen recognized the face: "It was Head Chef Grumbel. He went right through me."

Dink couldn't move...he was petrified, an emotion he rarely knew. Nothing had ever scared him that much...not even when the nurse at Lakeside administered the new polio vaccine to the students. Dink hated needles.

"**AAAHHH...AAAHHH...AAAHHH,**" Dink screamed.

He started to run toward the student activity that was flocking together on the school grounds. But, as he began to move, he felt something on top of one of his tennies: it was a muscular forefinger. He kicked the body part farther than any kickball that he had ever kicked for a home run on the kickball court. Instantly, a vigilant vulture dipped down from overhead, snatched the finger food, and flew off into the sunrise. The ugly bird came too close; Dink's nerves finally surrendered and he passed out.

Dink missed his morning engagement with the lovely Lorraine; instead, he had to intersect with her frightening father in the nurse's clinic.

"I can hardly wait; I'd rather swallow castor oil." Dink didn't reveal any information about the ghost story.

"What did you say? I didn't understand."

"Nothing. Nothing."

As Dink Playlen was recovering, he did get a visit from the object of his affection.

"My father is sending me to boarding school," Lorraine informed the patient as he recovered on the infirmary bed. "**What**?

Why? Whe...did he...he decide that?" The statement caught him completely off-guard.

"This morning."

"Where are you going?"

"Three Egg, up in the cold part of the state. Dink, I'm upset but I nee...I want to go."

"When are you leaving?"

"Tonight, on a jet plane—destination: 'Omelette Town.'"

Any possible Dink Playlen/Lorraine Coffery connection had just been snuffed out. Dink's heart was crushed, but his cherished Lorraine was relieved. "I'll let you go without a fight."

The Saint Petersburg cops were on the scene in a matter of hours. They had pulled the water-logged remains out of the lake. Principal Coffery and Mrs. Grumbel were also at water's edge.

The other three T&P officers and most of the student body watched the horrible event from the schoolhouse windows.

Link Playlen looked through the glass and wondered: "What's that long black bag on the ground?"

"It's a body bag," Tim answered. "Notice the zipper, huh?"

Later that day, the pupils, teachers, cafeteria staff, and maintenance workers were assembled in the auditorium.

"There's a rear end in every perch," Tim said, waving his hand over the large room.

"Aren't any no-shows for this little gathering," Link stated, "that's cool. How you feelin', Dink?"

"Awful, wait'll I tell you guys the new news."

Principal Coffery, with Mrs. Grumbel and the cops alongside, presided over the congregation. "The dead diver was Carl "Cookie" Steinberg. Believe me, no...body should be afraid. Carl shouldn't have jumped the fenc..."

A voice interrupted: "**How do you know he jumped the fence?**" Nobody could figure out who had spoken.

PegLeg ignored the question and continued: "Everybody should stay away from the lake and the gators."

The sheriff stepped in front of the principal and grabbed the microphone. "Believe me, if there was any foul play, we'll capture the culprit or culprits."

Again, a mysterious articulation: "**Sure you will!**"

Someone in the assembly said: "**Look!** There's an empty seat in the last row. Who was sitting there?" Not a soul could recall.

Carl Steinberg's favorite cookie had always been the Fig Newton—he usually had a bag in his blue-and-white hot rod, hence the nickname. The most disturbing fact to the T&P brotherhood was that Cookie was Kim Tender's boyfriend. She was Tim and Todd's only sister, the top sibling on the Tender totem-pole. Kim Tender had golden hair that she was always changing around. She would wear it up; wear it down; wear it in a ponytail. Sometimes, her hair would disappear underneath the ball cap that she enjoyed wearing.

Kim Tender also worked part-time in the concession at the Park Theater, the place she had met Carl Steinberg. He had been an usher. Cookie was also a "greaser," but he could seat people faster than when Gregory Peck flew his war planes in *Twelve O'Clock High*.

"I remember the night that Kim and Carl met," Todd said. "*A Double Life*, starring Ronald Colman and Shelley Winters was playing. A classic."

"Something in Saint Petersburg isn't kosher," Tim said, "seven people dead in a once peaceful neighborhood couldn't be a coincidence, huh?"

"This is getting too close to home," Link said.

"We need to schedule a meeting to discuss a very serious subject...a supernatural subject that has visited the T&P fellowship once too often," Todd said. "Do I hear a second?"

"I second," Tim said. He was squeezing the blue-and-yellow cloth that had become his constant companion.

"Good, then it's settled."

Chapter 8

It was late Monday afternoon and Kim Tender was in a state of sorrow. Tim Tender called home from school—Principal Coffery had not cancelled classes.

"How's Kim doing, Ma?"

"She's not good, Tim, but don't worry, we'll take care of her. Tell Todd not to worry, either."

Tim knew his sister was injured in her heart. He felt bad; he knew his twin felt the same.

"What about the funeral?"

"Kim doesn't want to go; said she wants to remember Carl full of life and not full of vulture holes. The Steinbergs did request that she sit *Shiva* with them. They've always said they love Kimmie like one of their own."

"What's *Shiva*?"

"It's a seven-day mourning period that Jewish people observe after the death of a loved one. As a custom, they have seven family members attend but now only six live in the area; so, they asked your sister."

"Did she agree?"

"Yes, she feels that it will help comfort her to grieve with his family. They told her not to wear any makeup and to bring a garment that she won't mind tearing."

"Why?"

"To symbolize her broken heart. We've arranged for her to take the time off from school." Kim attended Lakehood High, which was located across Lake Maggiore from Lakeside Elementary.

The Steinbergs had requested a quick autopsy, and the coroner found traces of carbon monoxide, as well as water, in Cookie's lungs; therefore, the actual cause of death had yet to be determined.

Carl Steinberg would be laid to rest at Cemetery Hill. Rabbi R. Serling was contacted to conduct the service, and he organized, with A. Hister, the delivery of the pine casket to the parlor. Mr. Hister was happy to help; besides, since his windfall of the Barrens' four-plus-one funerals, things had been rather minimal in the burying business. He had enjoyed the niceties that the extra money had afforded him.

"Timothy, we'll all go over and offer our respects some time before the following *Shabbat*," Tim sounded a little puzzled, "Saturday, the Jewish Sabbath. Okay?"

"Oh, that's right. Fine, Ma. I'll tell Todd."

Chapter 9

The school clock read four-forty-four, and the Tender and Playlen twins were starting their offhand meeting at the table located behind the last row of bookshelves in the back of the library. All the furniture in the "room of the classics" was honey maple—PegLeg's influence was far reaching.

The T&P President brought his mahogany mallet down on the tabletop: "Mr. Secretary, could you please read the minutes from the last meeting?"

"Gladly, Mr. President," Tim returned. He relayed information concerning the marvelous movie the gang had consumed last session. Tim withheld talk about the nightmarish scenes he had endured later that same evening. Permission would have to be granted. "Mr. President, can I discuss some new business?"

"Not at the present time. Mr. Treasurer, how much money remains in the T&P fund?"

"Let me count it, sir. Six dollars, three cents." Tim placed the money back in the Hav-A-Tampa cigar box that his father had gotten from Ybor City, a Spanish-Cuban community in Tampa, Florida, where many of the nation's cigars were produced. "The treasury is low since school started—not enough time to do the odd jobs to build it up."

"But," VP Link said, bouncing in his seat, not waiting to be acknowledged, "that's enough to get candy, cokes, and four tickets at the Florida Theatre and still have coins leftover jiggling in our pockets. In three weeks they're running a double feature: *Dracula's Daughter* and a new movie, *Creature from the Black Lagoon*."

The *Florida*, which was just south of Central Avenue on Fifth Street, was the fanciest of all the theaters downtown. And there were many movie houses to choose from in the bustling part of the city: the *Cameo*, the *State*, and the *Pheil* were just a few. The *Pheil* was unique—when a customer walked in, the screen was above the patron's head instead of at the end of the aisle, as it was in most cinema palaces.

The *Florida* was also a favorite retreat for local teenage couples. The building had two balconies...one on top of the other, and the highest area of armchairs contributed least to the light bill.

"Great," Tim added, "the decorations remind me of Camelot and King Arthur; Lady Guinevere; Sir Launcelot."

Dink spoke: "It reminds me of the Knights; the Round Table; Excalibur," the sergeant at arms raised his arm as if holding a sword.

Tim was pretending the opposite maneuver like he was pulling the legendary blade out of a rock.

"Merlin; and the enemies, Morgan le Fay and Sir Mordred are what I think of when I walk in the theater," Link said.

The boys were too excited to follow procedure. They had learned about the Arthurian Legend in one of Miss Tester's English lessons. She was a super teacher.

The president motioned for the remaining T&P members to sit down; then, brought them back to reality. "How can you think of that stuff after what took place this morning?"

"You're right; we're sorry."

"Do we need to review any old business?" the *Pres.* said.

"**No, sir!**"A firm *shoosh* came from the front desk where the librarian was standing, even though she couldn't see the gang.

"Are there any new topics that anyone wants to bring up?" Todd said. Right away a Tender arm and a Playlen arm reached toward the ceiling—Tim and Dink were connected to the kid-sized upper limbs.

"You first, Dink," President Tender said.

"Thank you, Mr. President. I forgot to tell you guys that when I saw Chef Grumbel at the lake, he didn't have anything below his right sleeve where his hand should have been."

"That means he hasn't found his forearm and hand that were missing from the accident," Link responded.

"Where the hell would he find them," Dink asked.

"On the *other side*, maybe, wherever that is," Link returned, pointing a finger upward. "How should I know?"

The president jumped into the conversation: "That'll be enough bickering, boys. Tim, you have the floor."

"I knew that I would have to bring this to light sooner or later." Even though he was reluctant to do so, Tim Tender had to revisit one of the most terrifying nights of his *young* life—a night that he hoped would stay a fantasy and not develop into reality. Of course, the object in the right side of his bluejeans might suggest otherwise. "....And that's what was written on all of our gravestones."

It was as if Todd, Link, Dink, and Tim were roasting around a raging campfire exchanging shocking stories about slippery ghosts; haunted houses on hills; and maniacs on the prowl. Only, it wasn't summer vacation at Camp Spartan... it was fall, fast into the current school year...and there was no fireside chatting going on in the library.

After the secretary/treasurer's next act of emotional cruelty, there was no need to continue the meeting. "Okay, you guys ready for this? What I have hidden in my pocket... that I'll take out if you want me to...you're not going to believe, huh?"

"Well, how're we going to know what it is, ass-wipe, if you don't show us?" Dink said, with a look of ridicule on his face.

"Yea, man, we can take it, we're not sissies," Todd added.

"Cool! let's have it," Link said.

The article that had previously been stuffed down in Tim's denim pants was now in the center of the conference table. It immediately became the focus of each T&P member's eyes: the deceased cub scout's blue-and-yellow scarf.

There was a motion brought to the floor, which was seconded three times: the time to contact Granny Hart had arrived.

Chapter 10

That Monday night at the Tender household things were pretty somber. The family members, except Kim, were all engaged in activities to try and take their minds off of the morning's tragedy. Kim was at the Steinbergs' home submerged deep into training for the start of *Shiva* on Tuesday.

Mom and Dad Tender were in their bedroom visiting with Everett, Jr., the baby brother that occupied the very bottom of the Tender totem-pole. He had sunrise-shaded red hair, the only one in the family with such a color. He didn't talk or walk yet. And for the other household members' peace of mind and body, he slept most of the night and didn't scream much.

All the older Tender kids, usually two-at-a-time, had the privilege of baby-sitting their infant brother when Mom and Dad Tender would go out dancing, usually on Thursday nights, at the casino in Gulfport, which was a little town west of St. Petersburg. They would get dressed in outfits that the other amateur hoofers seemed to always want to take snapshots of.

"Rod, come on, let me in, huh?" Tim pleaded, banging on the door to his teenaged brother's room, which was filled with car-racing posters and pictures of huge engines. "I want to play too."

"Sorry, forget it, Timmy; I have hotels on Boardwalk and Park Place, houses on all the greens and reds, and ownership of all four railroads. The only thing the Toad has is a hotel on Marvin Gardens and nothing on the other yellows. He'll be dead shortly and I'll ship him out in a box. Then maybe you can come in and challenge the 'ruler of real estate.'"

"The name's Todd not Toad." Todd had a look of game-playing despair on his face, his strategy was quickly approaching the surrender stage.

"I want to come in now and see the annihilation," Tim begged.

"Nope, can't do it."

"You better stop teasing and let me in. I'll tell Mom, huh?"

"Go ahead Timmy Wimmy." Rod stood firm. He would torment his younger siblings by only allowing one of them at a time into his room.

"Sometimes, you're a slug."

Tim wished Kim was home; she would let the young Tenders play in her area together, as long as they kept away from her new *45s*. Her bedroom was "Heartthrob Heaven" with banners of Frank Sinatra, Montgomery Clift, and Marlon Brando covering every available inch of the walls.

Tim Tender decided that he couldn't wait any longer. "This is useless." He wandered down the hall, entered his room, and gazed at his prized 1911 *Mutt and Jeff* Comic Book. Tim knew that it was one of the first comic books ever published and wanted it for his collection—found it at a garage sale of all places. But, instead of reading about Bud Fisher's tall and short funny guys with the top hats, he grabbed one of the terror version EC's—his favorites—a comic that not only had the Crypt-Keeper but the Vault-Keeper and the Old Witch on the cover.

But, again, he quickly changed his mind and went with his copy of *The Martian Chronicles*, the wonderful stories of science fiction about the red planet. Ray Bradbury was one of his most beloved authors. Tim began to entertain himself.

All of Tim's books were placed on the shelves in succession starting with the very first one he ever savored, Henry James's *The Turn of the Screw*, to the most recent work enjoyed, *The Old Man and the Sea*, by the reigning Nobel Prize Winner for Literature, Ernest "Papa" Hemingway.

After luxuriating in the chapter labeled "April 2005: Usher II*," Tim Tender was dropping into a nice sleep, his head moving slowly in the direction of his down pillow. Just as he was nodding off, he glanced at his alarm clock, "It's midnight! Mister Bradbury's written a fine tribute to Poe's, *The Cask of Amontillado*. I wonder if revenge plays a part in the Saint Petersburg killings? It's late. Todd's not here yet. Quite a long Monopoly game."

Oddly enough, Tim didn't suffer a nightmare that evening, even after—in his reader's mind—existing within the dark, dank catacombs and feeling the deadly claustrophobia that befell *Mr. Garret* after *Stendahl's* bricklaying escapade. Tender slept peacefully.

Chapter 11

It was Tuesday afternoon, after an extremely strained day at Lakeside Elementary, and school kids had stayed home in droves.

Each member of the T&P club had attended, but now they were pedaling their Schwinn *Travelers* toward the Granny Hart mansion. Their wish was to gain some information about a killer by contacting a dead cub scout. The streets in the area were brick, not red but pink—no one in town ever knew why. Granny's place was located on one of the lost lanes: Demens Drive.

The manor was a cream-colored, two-story job that rested on top of a leveled-off mound next to the sacred Timucan Indian burial grounds, which were located at the very southern tip of the city called St. Petersburg.

The Florida-style family room of the home faced the water of Tampa Bay. French doors consisting of green-colored wood and slightly-tinted windows decorated the east and west sides of the estate.

The yard, mostly weeds either sprouting up or spreading out, stretched about fifty yards from the home to the waterfront. The beach's muddy strand reached forth and came face-to-face with the small, white-capped waves of the bay. This inlet location didn't have any of the fluffy white sand found on the shores of the Gulf of Mexico, which sometimes reminded the *snowbirds* visiting from the North of freshly-fallen snow. If a *tourista* took a stroll on Granny's shore, his or her feet would instantly sink as if they were engulfed in shallow quicksand.

"You know, Rod, Stinky, and some of their friends have been here a few times. Granny tol d them that she likes things dark,"

Tim said. The boys dropped their red, white, and blue bikes on the curb.

"I heard she doesn't like girls much." Dink stared at the red gate that led to a basement, a scarce find in Florida. "Do you think she has a dungeon down there?"

"Cool," Link responded, "maybe there's locks and chains."

"Hey, man, how about a *rack*?" Todd added.

Tim immediately got a tingling sensation in his arms and legs. "Let's go, huh?" He started up the long walkway to the horse-shoe-arched door. The others followed slowly.

"That's really dark wood; I wonder what kind it is?" Dink said.

Tim commented: "I hope six dollars and three cents will cover any cost involved, huh?"

"I'm not really looking forward to communicating with dead people," Link said, examining the yard, "there sure is a lot of weeds."

"Who is?" Todd responded.

"We have to. What other choice do we have, huh?" Tim questioned.

The two sets of twins were now in such a determined mind set that Dink forgot to resolve what kind of lumber the portal was. They finally reached the top of the steep slope. One of the Tenders, Todd, grabbed the gold-metal knocker, pulled it back, and banged it forward on the gold-metal plate.

"Who's out there?" Granny cried.

"We're brothers and friends of Rod Tender," Tim yelled.

"I think she's hard of hearing."

"Oh, Roddy! He's such a nice, scampish young man. Wait just a second and let me unlatch my dead bolts, I have four of them, you know."

Each lock was separated from its holder. Granny pulled back the heavy door with both hands.

None of the twins had ever seen her. After Harvey, her husband, had died, she never left the mansion...even had her groceries delivered in.

After the door opened to its capacity, a short, round woman with pink cheeks stood unevenly in the middle of the corridor.

Immediately, Tim noticed Granny's passed-the-hips, dirty gray hair. Todd noticed the red streaks on her knee-length, stained white apron. Dink noticed her ankle-length, soiled blue dress. Link noticed her big toe sticking out of her right tennis shoe. Mrs. Hart's sneakers were Keds, red ones, just like his—Link realized that there was some common ground to work with:

"Cool shoes, Granny Hart," Link said with enthusiasm.

She smiled, a big smile, exposing two solid-gold crowns where the front teeth used to be. "Oh, thank you, young man. The shoes were a present from dear Harvey—six years ago on my sixty-second birthday; he died later that year. I never take them off, you know, not even when I wash up."

"Man, don't they get wet?" Todd questioned.

"It's no big deal, I only bathe once a month," she said as she scratched her stringy hair.

"Shit! no wonder it smells in here," Dink said.

"What did you say, young man?" the old woman said, wearing a pungent air about her like a halo.

"He didn't say a thing, Mrs. Hart," Tim said as he turned toward Dink, "watch it, that cursing won't help us gain her assistance."

"Come into the kitchen. I'm preparing some wonderful meatless *marinara*, with giant, juicy tomatoes that I grew in my own garden. **And**! it's loaded with bits of fresh garlic and diced Vidalia onions. I got the onions from a lovely couple, the Spencer, Jrs., that I met while visiting Snellville, Georgia, with Harvey before he passed on. Would you boys like to stay for dinner?"

The kids remembered the weeds and looked at each other with puzzled expressions, wondering how anything edible could have grown in that patch of ground. And, how old could those onions have been before entering the sauce? They didn't respond right away to her question about the eats.

Because of the extreme darkness in the long, skinny hall that led to the room that included sauce, the kitchen sink, and, shortly, a nut, each member of the T&P club bounced off the walls on the way.

"Hey, Granny, how the hell do you see in this joint?" Dink asked. He was rapidly knocking off the offensive one-liners.

"Just hold on to my apron and follow me boys, I feel that the supper is bubbling."

The twins and Granny stood around the greasy General Electric stove in such a manner that a Tender-Hart-Playlen sandwich was formed.

As they watched her stir, the boys saw what looked like cockroaches pushing up from the bottom of the copper cooking pot passed the surface of the spaghetti sauce. The kids also detected numerous smaller chunks of something dark floating around—doubtless flies. Link said later that he thought he saw a kamikaze housefly jump from the shelf above the stovetop and splash the red stuff—a perfect "cannonball." The boys didn't even want to know about the noodles.

"It's perfect; you boys gather around the table and I'll dish it up," Granny said with glee.

"For the sake of the cause, let's sit down and take our lumps," Tim whispered to the other kids.

"This is actually pretty good grub, Granny Hart," Link commented, "it has a nice crunch."

His brother responded: "Yea, real tasty!" He turned and hissed under his breath, "Link, are you cracked?"

"How 'bout some dessert, boys?"

"Oh, I'm full," Tim said patting his stomach, "couldn't eat another bite."

"Me too."

"Same here."

Link jumped up from the kitchen chair, "I'll have some."

While he was finishing Granny's "sweet surprise," the other banquet guests and Mrs. Hart moved carefully into the parlor which faced Tampa Bay.

The seance room contained tall burgundy curtains; fancy sconces; a fancier chandelier; and the fanciest item of all—a beautiful jukebox.

And, the "table of the dearly departed"—the one where visitors from the *other side* described things only a handful of the living could digest—occupied the very center of the dead space.

Mrs. Hart was a clairvoyant—had completed a home correspondence course. She had graduated two years back from the Palmetto School of Psychics. She was the valedictorian of her senior class, and the honor was well-deserved because she knew about the award long before the professors told her. She was never invited to any alumni functions. In her parting address—sent via a reel-to-reel—she blurted out that the chancellor of Palmetto U., in the next calendar year, was going to embezzle the contributions that were collected every spring semester for the retired psychics of the twin cities of Saint Petersburg and Palmetto. It turns out that she was wrong....Chancellor Chuck Chuklehed was actually fired for running an illegal dice game on university property.

Granny had decided to become a clairvoyant after her loving husband, Harvey, had died from a rare disease, *amyotrophic lateral sclerosis.* She wanted to be able to visit with him and console and be consoled.

The Harts, when Harvey was alive, were happiest when they performed together in the U.S.O. Camp Shows during *W.W.II,* mostly in the Pacific Islands, entertaining the homesick soldiers. Granny played the alto oboe, and Harvey did his *turn* on the piccolo. Their two most requested tunes were both Irving Berlin compositions: "Alexander's Ragtime Band" and "God Bless America." They felt best about their productions when they were able to put smiles on the faces of the boys that were lying in the military hospitals, mutilated—some for life—by the war. The songs seemed to ease the soldiers' miseries, if only briefly, and it gave the Harts a purpose for *their* lives, even though it was difficult to perform amidst all the pain and suffering.

After Mr. Hart passed away, Mrs. Hart realized that she could earn a pittance from her other-world talent. Granny started taking outside business. But, a mistake during a call-back session put a stop to her spirit-chasing. Since that disaster, the only other-world inhabitant she contacted was her loving husband.

"**Burp!** Man, that was great grub, Granny Hart," Todd said, trying to keep whatever it was that had just traveled down his throat from coming up. He was happy that Mom Tender didn't use Granny's recipe for her Italian sauce.

"Todd, that's awful," Tim said, as he, Todd, and Dink settled in around the callback table. "Mrs. Hart, we would like to appeal to your sense of compassion and justice and beg you to return to the job that you did so well in the past."

"I'm sorry boys, but I haven't engaged in any recall business since the Bea E. Hopkins problem."

"What the hell ya going on about, Granny?" Dink said.

"What problem?" Tim asked. "Watch it, Dink." Tender shot eye darts in his buddy's direction.

"Roddy, Warren, and their friend, Densel, brought that girl to the house one day. I don't like the female types so much, you know." She flung her hands in the air in a kind of prissy manner.

"Bea's a star softball player on the Lakehood High Spartan team; she's great," Todd added, "bats cleanup." He swung an imaginary bat.

"And Densel works at Aunt Hattie's as a broiler cook," Tim added, "Dad's favorite restaurant."

"Right!" Granny said, "Can I continue? Anyway, Bea wanted to contact her hero, the legendary George Herman Ruth. They call him the 'Babe,' you kn..."

"Yea, we know," Todd chimed in.

"Boys! you must stop interrupting. Anyway, Bea wanted to ask Mr. Ruth if he could help her with her power stroke. She had always been fascinated with the story about when the 'Babe' supposedly hit a foul ball on top of the West Coast Inn across from the Al Lang ballpark in downtown St. Pete."

"We know where it is!"

"Boys, please! Anyway, Mr. Hart and I met Mr. Ruth once, you know. Bea also wished that she could visit, one day, 'the house that Ruth built,' Yankee Stadium, and actually experience the place where he hit many of his *714* Herculean shots."

"Sounds like you're a pretty big fan, too, Granny," Tim said patting his twin on the back, "Todd, bet you would've liked to have been here for that seance, huh?"

"You better believe it, man. Maybe he would've given me his autograph."

"No signatures that night, unfortunately," Granny said.

"Instead of communicating with the Yankee champion, I mistakenly brought back some bleacher bum that was eating a candy bar and drinking red wine from a shopping bag. He was also wearing a NY Yankee ball cap. The wino kept repeating, 'Hey, Bambino, hit it outa here.' After the old drunk offered Bea a sip of his rot gut at the same time he was waving a fancy pocket knife, Miss Hopkins shot out of here faster than a bullet from a *Ladysmith* .38 Special. Then, I became the laughing stock of the community, so I quit. So, boys, as you can see, I just can't help you."

The boys were persistent; they felt it was important to connect with the dead cub scout and find out any information possible about *their* ghostly visitor.

"But Granny Hart, you've got to be *cool*, as my brother would say; by the way, where is he? Don't you have to help us, *huh*, as Tim would say? *Man*, as Todd would say, isn't it the right thing to do?"

"I'm sorry, but I've got to make an important call and talk to someone I miss very much." Mrs. Hart stood up. "You come back Sunday on Halloween, after dark. If you want to discuss any summons to the 'unliving,' bring six dollars, three cents. That's what it cost for the initial session. Also, if you can, bring something that belonged to the individual that you want to contact."

Tim Tender had the perfect item—it was blue-and-yellow.

As the three kids got back to their bicycles, they realized that they were missing a T&P member: it was Link. The president, the sergeant at arms, and the secretary/treasurer retrieved the vice president—the perfect dinner guest. Each boy, except Link, while heading for his particular medicine cabinet, concocted a scheme to get out of eating the evening meal at home.

Chapter 12

That night, Tim and Todd, having been surprised about Granny's agreement to communicate with Eddie Liebowitz on Halloween, were too wound up to sleep. They decided to talk about the family's favorite restaurant and some of the things they liked best about it.

"Tim, what's your favorite food at Aunt Hattie's?" Todd sat up on his twin bed.

"No contest, *Chicken 'N' Dumplings*," Tim also sat up and swung his feet off the bed onto the floor. "Densel told me once how they prepare it and that it's very popular with the Northerners."

"How do they fix it?"

Both the boys already knew everything about what they were in the process of discussing but were trying to gain entry into the corridors of *snoozeville*.

"It's made with a melt-in-your-mouth, one-quarter baked chicken; oversized, fluffy dumplings laced with yellow gravy made from scratch with the drippings of the chicken; and baby green peas sprinkled over the entire meal. It's enough food for two of me to eat." Two of his fingers formed a "V."

"Man, I could go for some right now," Todd said, after smacking his lips.

"Densel also told me that the owners, Aunt Hattie, her husband, Uncle Ed, and their son, Frank—the Boore family—consider it one of the 'signature' dishes," Tim said. "What's your prime choice, Todd?"

"That's it, brother."

"What's it?"

"Slow-roasted *prime rib* with *au jus* sauce made from the fat and juices from the beef—like the chicken drippings used for your yellow gravy. And, the cooks take sea salt, fresh ground pepper, and chopped garlic and rub the seasonings into the meat under the fat lip that covers it, which makes it even tastier. Densel said that he's responsible for that prep task and has to squeeze lemon juice on his hands at end of his shift to get the garlic smell off. Then, the final step: the chefs cook 'em lazily overnight to hold in the most flavor—man, that's good eatin'."

"Who told you all that?"

"Dennnnsellll. He can also broil those steaks and chops like a mad man." Todd turned his wrist as if flipping a piece of meat.

"What kind of side dish do you like best with your beef?" Tim asked his twin.

"Well, you order a steamin' hot, flaky, baked Idaho tater smothered with tons of butter, sour cream, and chives," Todd made a sprinkling gesture; "then, use crumbled bacon to top it all off."

"I like the bacon crispy, not fatty," Tim added. "Sounds like a feast fit not only for the King but the Queen and all their royal Subjects."

Instead of bringing the twins drowsiness, all the gab about the great grub made them hungry. A late-night snack was in order.

The twins tiptoed down the hallway, passed the dining room, into the kitchen, and went directly to the refrigerator. Then, they set the table.

"Man, I love peanut butter," Todd removed his finger from the Skippy jar, "Tim, pass me a slice, will ya? From the half without the anchovies."

Tim was popping marshmallows in his mouth and couldn't answer but passed a piece of pizza sans the little fish. He then mixed, in a brown bowl, the sweet treats with the slimy ones that he picked off the Italian pie and dug in.

"That's awful, Tim; you must be the only person I know who can stand anchovies. And that's a good way to ruin marshmallows."

"I do love anchovies, huh. Besides, it's like eating caviar compared to Granny's *bug fare*."

"I know, I know; we almost used the whole bottle of bicarbonate of soda when we got home. You know what else Densel told me?"

"What?"

"That during some of the years of World War II, because the restaurant's interior only contained sixteen seats, the Boores would cart box lunches of hamburgers, homemade pie, and *chicken-in-the-woodpile...*"

"That's French fries."

"I know, don't interrupt."

"Sorry." Tim made a zipper motion over his lips.

"Anyway. They took the food up to the soldiers staying at the Vinoy Park Hotel, the Soreno and the Detroit."

"What about the Suwannee Hotel?"

"Densel said they used the Suwannee's beds for the commercial customers, not as military bunks. At one point, according to Densel, there were over 39,000 draftees in town."

"How'd they fit them all downtown?"

"Many of them had to set up temporary residence in a "Tent City" west of here—the Jungle area of St. Petersburg."

"Out near the Gulf of Mexico, huh?"

"Right. Others were taken north to Clearwater. They stayed in places like the Fort Harrison, which in 1947 became the spring home of the Philadelphia Phillies. They also took some soldiers to the Belleview Biltmore."

"You know, Todd, the Biltmore is acclaimed to be the world's largest inhabited wooden structure."

"I didn't know that."

"Miss Tester told me!"

"Your sweetie!" Todd couldn't hold back a chuckle.

"Stuff it!" Tim tenderly socked his twin's shoulder.

About fifteen minutes later, both their heads hit the pillows and traveled to *slumberville*.

Chapter 13

Halloween had finally arrived.

The Tender and Playlen twins were standing in the dressing room at E. A. Poe's Costume Emporium. Link had brought his getup from home.

"It's great that your dad is able to lend us the outfits for free," Tim said, as he was pulling a mask over his head. His *Mummy* was complete...he wanted to go as *Frankenstein*, but they were all gone. He stared at the mirror. "Perfect." He walked out of the fitting room; Todd followed as *Count Dracula* with Dink's *Wolf Man* riding the bloodsucker's formal tails.

"I didn't shave for three weeks to make my costume look more realistic." Dink rubbed his chin.

They stood in the outer chamber, where empty hangers hung on the racks that earlier held wardrobe after wardrobe of trick-or-treat garb.

"Where's Link?" Todd asked.

"He's still working on his *Army* costume," Dink answered, putting his thumb up like a hitchhiker in the direction of the dressing closet.

"I thought you two were going as twin werewolves?" Tim said.

"That was the original plan; but, now he says he's got something else in mind; he's not going to Granny Hart's until later—says he has some unfinished business to take care of first," Dink said rolling his eyes, "I'll let him explain."

"Because the rentals are free-of-charge, we'll have all the money for the seance," the treasurer said as he retrieved the coins from the *panatela* holder. "Dink, will your dad look after this box? Don't want to lose it."

Dink took the cigar box. "Sure."

Link finally made his exit looking like one of General George Patton's brave warriors: olive-drab khakis; netted Army helmet—red beanie underneath; and belt containing a dented canteen in a case opened at the top end.

"I'm ready for Coffery."

The other boys decided not to chase the explanation of that statement.

They wanted to leave early—before going to Granny's—and get some time logged for "Trick-or-Treat" candy. Even though it was still daylight, lots of Saint Petersburg residents would be sitting and waiting for little *Ghosts and Goblins*. And, there were already loads of parents roaming the neighborhoods for added precaution.

The T&P *candy*, *apple*, and *candy-apple* tour always began at the Tenders' house on Twenty-fifth Street; continued north to Tangerine Avenue; headed east to Twenty-second Street—one block shy of Chimera Road; turned south to Lakeview Avenue, circled back to the west; and finished with a walk north to where they started.

After separating the good from the bad goodies in their brown grocery bags, the T&P membership grabbed their red, white, and blue bikes and, with the exception of Link, peddled toward the paranormal den meeting, hopefully, with the deceased cub scout.

They fashioned a one-from-four split; Link had two more stops on his last-day-of-October trip: his pad and Principal Deacon Coffery's place. *Claude* and *Christine* Playlen were attending a masquerade ball that evening at the Gulfport Casino and wouldn't be home. The Playlens were double-dating with Tim and Todd's mom and dad, who were going as Harpo and Groucho Marx.

Link streaked to his house.

* * *

Inside the pink palace, the vice president replaced his treats with some tricks: five rolls of toilet paper—one for each time Coffery's "holy paddle," alias *Alois,* had become familiar with Link's *red rum*p. He also grabbed a flashlight, a book of matches from Warren's room, a large spoon, and another tan shopping bag from the kitchen...just in case he found a surprise on his route-to-revenge. Link Playlen didn't forget easily. **And**! in the morning on All Saints' Day, the Northern Maple trees in PegLeg's front yard would contain limbs covered with mysterious, white paper leaves. After completing his unfinished business, Link would meet his brother and his best friends at Granny Hart's.

Chapter 14

"**Who's out there**?" yelled Granny Hart.

"**It's us again, friends of Rod Tender. You told us to come back on Halloween night, remember?**"

"Oh, Roddy! He's such a delightfully devilish boy. Wait just a minute and let me unlock my dead bolts; I have four of them, you know; although, I seem to have only locked three tonight." She pulled back the bulky door and there stood *Count Dracula*, the *Mummy*, and the *Wolf Man*. "Oh, wonderful, trick-or-treaters, you're my first. I have some lovely beetles from my backyard that I prepared with a nice chocolate coating. I was afraid that I was going to have to eat all the delicious morsels myself, and I need to watch my girlish figure, you know." She shoved a plastic pumpkin near the boys' faces.

Another sacrifice to the "cause" for three-quarters of the T&P membership. As the guys were licking and crunching, Tim said, "Yum! these are great, Granny, but we should save some for Link, he'll be here shortly."

"You know, you shouldn't talk with food in your mouth, young man. Besides, you can't enjoy the full flavor of the little buggies. You boys go into the front room; I'm going to change into my Halloween wardrobe. This is a special day for Harvey and I— our golden anniversary. We were married on October 31, 1904. I'm happy that you boys are here to celebrate with us."

"Obviously she's forgotten about contacting Eddie Liebowitz for us," Todd said—disappointment overtaking his mug like a mask.

"Well, we'll remind her after we attend the fifty-year celebration," Tim said, being his usual, practical— sometimes self-admitted—boring self.

"Sounds like a damn fine time," Dink added, rubbing his hands together hard enough to start a fire.

As Todd, Tim, and Dink walked toward the "chamber of the departed," they heard a tune playing beyond the French doors. The kids had to step down into the sunken room. There was a jukebox in the corner rendering a style of music that Tim recognized immediately: it was *bebop* performed in fine fashion by Charlie Parker. *Jazz* was Tim's favorite class of music.

"That 'Yardbird' can sound that sax, can't he?" Tim said. "At first I thought that juke was a big garbage can."

"Yea, man, 'Bird's' great," Todd responded, "that music machine Granny has is the *S-148* that the Seeburg Company came out with in 1948. And, you're right, Tim, they call the box the 'trash can' or the 'barrel' because of its shape. Also, Seeburg was the first to come up with a juke after the war, the *S-146*. Our government made the jukebox manufacturers produce only war-related material from 1942 to 1946."

The song player was made with a blond-colored wood and metal cabinet, a white fluted dome, and a red cylinder running down each side. Tim knew music, but Todd understood music machines and their history.

"Crap, Dizzy's better," Dink said. "When he blows his horn, he looks like a damn chipmunk with a cheek full of berries." Dink made his own cheeks look like twin balloons. "Granny's table is mahogany—nice, rich-looking finish. That chair is also a mahogany grain."

There were four other chairs, all folding-style, leaning against a wall. The three boys each retrieved a chair, and Dink set up a fourth for Link, trusting that he would show soon.

Directly overhead the mid-area of the "desk of the deceased" was a lighted chandelier with eight separate lamps branching out from its core...each holding so many cobwebs that every spider in St. Petersburg must have left a donation.

"You know what's amazing," Tim dragged his finger across the shiny wood as if he had a white glove on, "the table, chair, and the crystal ball are the only things in here that don't have any dust or spider webs all over them."

"You're right," Todd put his hand on his chin, "weird, very weird."

There were eight sconces—evenly-spaced in the chamber—containing candles that were already burning.

The back middle of the room accommodated a fancy fireplace that had an angelic portrait in a circular frame over the mantel: newlyweds playfully smearing wedding cake all over each other's face.

"You think the pastry recipe for that cake contained any type of insect, Granny's favorite ingredient?" Tim amused. No one answered.

In the oil painting, Harvey was donning formal wear— all in brilliant white—that included a bowknot tie, shirt, cummerbund, pants, and patent leather shoes. Mrs. Hart was sporting an ivory-colored, silk wedding gown, beautifully-trimmed in frilly lace. They both appeared very happy.

Todd walked over to the juke to try and find some W. C. Handy, so he could hear some *blues*.

Dink spoke: "I wonder if it would be possible for me to visit Lorraine in Three Egg? Todd, is there any Vaughn Monroe? Play 'My Devotion' if it's on there; it's Lorraine's favorite."

Tim started to daydream:

Tim Tender walked into Denington's Grocery and Soda Shop, a popular Saint Petersburg hangout, to pick up some items for Mom Tender. He went to the front of the building, where the cleaning products were stored. After searching for a few minutes, he glanced in the direction of the soda fountain.

"What the...what are they doing here together?" Link and Lorraine were in the back sharing a single soda, each sipping from a separate straw, reminding Tender of lovebirds. Lorraine turned to the WurliTzer Jukebox on the table and dropped in a nickel.

On that crushing afternoon at Denington's, Tim slipped out before Link or Lorraine could see him—his confidence shaken. He wondered, briefly, if Link had told Lorraine that he was Dink. Tim never mentioned his sighting to Dink.

Then, the attention in Tim's mind shifted to the occasion when Miss Coffery, one glorious day, had kissed him on the left cheek, after Tim had towed her home from school.

Tim Tender came back to the present when "St. Louis Blues" began to blast from Mrs. Hart's Seeburg.

In the next instant, Granny entered the room wearing the identical matrimonial dress shown in the picture, strolling as if she was coming down the aisle for the first time. She was a vision of elegance—even with the red Keds at the bottom of her ensemble. The boys were pleasantly astonished.

* * *

Deacon Coffery inhabited the massive stone chateau on Serpentine Circle—a dead-end street—about a mile southeast of Demens Drive. It was the only structure of its kind in St. Petersburg and was built in the sixteenth century by Hernando de Soto, then governor of Cuba, and his followers, who in 1539 set out on an expedition to the peninsula between the Atlantic Ocean and the Gulf of Mexico.

Link hid his Schwinn in some bushes on Coffery's street, away from the house. He crept toward the mansion. The wind was kicking in; the air at dusk was inviting the coldness to join the scene.

On the course to his trick-and-ultimate-treat trip, Link noticed a Saint Bernard doing some business in an empty field—the entire block, with the exception of PegLeg's house, was nothing but barren plots. "Perfect, just what I was hoping for; this is going to be great."

Link waited patiently for the big pup's departure; then, he bolted to the waste area; scooped up the heap of steamy dog dung; and carefully placed the mess in his bag. "I have to remember to wash this spoon before I put in back in the kitchen drawer." Young Playlen's blueprint was now complete, all the materials had been delivered in divine fashion.

Darkness was sluggishly embracing St. Petersburg. Link's calm had to be tested a little longer—flashes of the "bashing board" easily slid into his head. "Okay, Coffery, it's time for payback for you and your wooden friend!"

The excitement of retaliation burned his insides, and he missed the arrival of the night's peak blackness. He crooked his head back and fixed his eyes on the moon, which was only showing enough to make it look like a lunar squint. The small sliver of moonlight actually visible was beaming down on a weather vane, which had the "N" and "W" prongs broken and only the "S" and "E" spikes in their primitive state. If not for the scanty shine of a single street lamp near Coffery's estate, being blind on this evening wouldn't have been a disadvantage.

VP Playlen was now posted on a thin sidewalk across the road from Deacon Coffery's mausoleum, gazing at the icy-looking steel door. He pointed his flashlight in the direction of the house.

"That's odd." Link was staring at a black wreath that encircled the black door knocker. "Christmas decorations almost two months before Christmas?" Then, he remembered that it was, after all, Halloween. The large portal had a greyish-green finish with mildew spots everywhere. On either side of the door was a large window with square panes. The granite-colored curtains were drawn.

"Those are miserable-looking creatures," Link said as he saw that on the eaves—like bookends—were a pair of beasts with buggy eyes; pointed ears; and sharp-looking claws. The grotesque figures rested in a crouching position, as if waiting to pounce on an innocent passer-by.

Link sensed that he had been standing and staring at PegLeg's for what seemed like an eternity, so he tried to move, but his feet felt like they were stuck in wet cement. He began to realize that not one kid had stopped by for a "treat." And, even though he had the "trick" department accounted for, after studying Principal Coffery's, he was getting second thoughts about concluding his mission.

"This place looks evil." Then, again, reflections of *Alois* penetrated his brain like a hot stitching needle; he became more determined to finish what he had started.

He moved across the pavement in zigzag fashion, stopping occasionally to search left to right, then front to back, like a soldier advancing into enemy territory.

"Alright Coffery, these are for you!"

The *first* toilet-paper bomb flew through the frigid wind and made a direct hit on one of Coffery's Northern Maples—the roll unraveled and white tissues trickled down like perfectly-dropped snow. The tree to the immediate right was the *second* victim, and the tissue landed by way of a passionate toss, that had Bob "Fastball" Feller seen it, he would have probably consulted Link for some pointers. The *third* and *fourth* butt-wiping grenades struck their mark on the two timbers that were next in the lineup. Link really came alive with the *fifth* and final fling of paper vindication.

"Take that!"

He started toward the doorstep with the Saint Bernard's contribution to his chicanery. Link Playlen was on a fast roll now. He charged the steel doorway; dropped the poop bag on the cement; pulled out the matches; and bent down to light the crappy mess. Instantly, the curtains in the window to the left flew open and a giant body appeared behind them.

Blam! the metal gateway withdrew with a titanic force, and someone or something grabbed Link's neck and pulled him into PegLeg's pit.

"Aaaaahhhhh!"

Chapter 15

Link Playlen started to sweat, even though the air in the room felt icy. He was getting scared. He was lying in a silk-lined, cushioned coffin. He could barely move six inches, up or down, right or left. There were grooved nails—so many he couldn't count them—reaching downward from the ceiling of the casket ending just above Link's body. He had thin streams of blood on his face as a result of moving his head. The small holes that had been cut into the death box helped him inhale and exhale despite the film of smoke in the area.

"Where am I? What am I doing in here? Am I dead? What is going on? **Help! Help! Somebody please help me!**"

His screams seemed to go unheard. But, there was someone listening.

Knock! Knock! Knock! Link's ears started to ring from the earsplitting thumps on the top of the casket. He began to realize that he could be in danger. He didn't think Principal Coffery would take the prank so seriously. "Who's out there?" Link said reluctantly.

"It is me, your *Kommandant*," Coffery said excitedly. "I was cheerfully surprised at your arrival. You should've let me know that you were coming, I could've been more prepared. Are you enjoying the barracks, master Playlen? I built your bunk myself out of honey maple, and another just like it. Oh, by the way, I have your flash lamp, Army helmet, and beanie. Would you like them?"

Link then heard barking just outside his padded prison chamber. "What's that awful howling?"

"Oh, that's my German shepherd. I call him 'Herr Wolf'—he can't wait to make your acquaintance. He's been a big help to me in my work. I think you may have hurt his feelings with your statement about his singing." Coffery removed the padlock from the coffin.

The piercing pokers began to retreat from Link's view, and there stood Deacon Coffery, all six-foot-three inches of him, in *dress* unlike what Link was wearing. This was an outfit resembling the type that he had studied about in one of Miss Tester's World History lessons dealing with the German Army Machine.

PegLeg leaned down slightly, and Link saw that most of his greasy hair was covered by a peaked visor cap that had four distinctive features: a silver eagle perched on top of a swastika; an aluminum-colored skull 'n' crossbones; a silver oakleaf wreath; and a gold cord that stretched from one side of the hat to the other, just slightly longer than the scar that ranged most of Coffery's face. PegLeg bent farther down, put his nose on Link's nose, and spoke—Link received the full power of Coffery's dragon breath, mostly caused by the Kool he had recently had in his mouth, now resting loosely between his left thumb and forefinger.

"Do you like my Halloween costume?" Coffery forced Link to sit up, which was difficult for the twin considering the handcuffs he was sporting. Coffery removed the restraints just long enough to take his prisoner's khaki shirt off.

In the background, a Disney song was playing on some sort of phonograph—Coffery began to hum the harmony. Then he began to sing, "Who's afraid of the big bad wolf, the big bad wolf, the big bad wo....Do you like my crooning?"

"Wonderful." Link could now see that the collar the Alsatian was modeling had been attached to a chain, which was sitting in a circular clump. He also noticed that the dog's chompers were locked in a position that suggested play: foul play.

Suddenly, *Kommandant* Coffery positioned himself into a frozen-like state, standing with his right leg concealed up to the knee by a black boot and linked to his wooden limb, as if they were glued with Elmer's. Also, his right arm and hand extended out-and-up toward the swastika that was tacked to the ceiling.

Coffery was clothed in a greyish-green, highly-decorated uniform. It seemed like he was getting ready to march in a Nazi parade. The medals above the left pocket were not the U.S. Purple Heart and the Silver Star—the ones he had proclaimed to the townspeople to have earned in the war. A gold knotted ribbon extended from Coffery's right shoulder to his right breast, where it was pinned by an iron cross.

"*Heil* Hitler!" Coffery spoke the terrible phrase as if *Der Fuehrer* was standing right in front of him.

Link Playlen was witnessing a side of his school's principal that he knew nothing about. Most of the kids at Lakeside Elementary felt PegLeg was cruel; but, was he crazy too?

As Link was staring at *Herr* Wolf's teeth, PegLeg limped to the record player, put on some marching music, and began to *goose* step in a very clumsy manner until the Nazi hymn was complete. Coffery came back to the coffin, pushed his captive down and stated, "I've got a pleasant surprise for you later, Playlen. You're shivering, I'll turn up the heat. Oh, by the way, here's a little present." He carefully placed the Saint Bernard grab bag next to Link's face. The last thing that young Playlen saw, as the death lid was closing, was that dreadful, red-white-and-black banner.

* * *

"Are you boys ready to meet my dear Mr. Hart?" Mrs. Hart questioned. "How do I look, do you think he'll be pleased?"

"Man, you look lovely," Todd returned. "I'm sure Mr. Hart will be extremely happy, but there is one favor I'd like to ask you, if I may? Woul...?"

The jukebox stopped playing. Granny walked passed her ceremonial chair to a dusty table that was sitting in the opposite corner from the record machine. She turned on a radio that was resting on the table top, tuned the dial to a station that had soft music, and returned to her fancy seat. Todd had earlier told Tim and Dink that the radio was a Philco *230* model. "Red Roses for a Blue Lady" was playing on the airwaves until it was interrupted by a news flash:

Glinda Grumbel...longtime Lakeside custodian...has been arrested for the brutal murder of local teenager, Carl "Cookie" Steinberg. We at station W.A.R.T. have learned from St. Petersburg's Sheriff, John Daniels, that he and Deputy Jack Walker, handcuffed, then drove...red lights flashing, sirens blaring...Mrs. Grumbel to police headquarters, where she remains in a jail cell pending further investigation. We at station W.A.R.T. will update you when we receive more information on this breaking story.

"Can you believe that?" Tim said as he was struggling out of his chair.

"Those clowns arrested Mrs, Grumbel." Todd said sarcastically.

"Damn morons!" Dink added.

Granny didn't even hear the bulletin...she was preparing herself to contact Harvey and start their golden celebration.

Suddenly, the lights of the chandelier went dark, the French doors on the sunset-side of the room flew open, the curtains pushed back, and something resembling a tornado started to circle the Florida room. It was moving so fast, none of the kids could tell what it was—as it proceeded by each sconce, the candle flame blew out.

Mrs. Hart began to yell, **"Harvey, Harvey, is that you**? What's the matter, are you angry that I wore my wedding dress? Are you upset about the shoes, should I have worn the heels?"

In an instant, the Philco *230* started to play familiar song lyrics:

All I want for Christmas is my two front teeth, my two front teeth, my two front teeth.

The whirlwind knocked the radio off the table onto the floor. The next item sacrificed was the Seeburg *S-148*, and records were broken faster than when Jesse Owens, the legendary runner, won his four gold medals in the 1936 Olympics, held in Berlin, Germany. Then the ghostly twister departed through the unopened French doors on the east end of the room. Immediately, the eight arms of the electric candelabrum lit up. All human eyes in the chamber, even Granny Hart's, focused on the pearl-handled knife that had spread clear glass on the "table of the dead." It was stuck in the middle of the crystal ball's foundation, straight up and down.

"What the hell was that?" Dink said.

"Man, that was eerie," Todd added.

"That's the same blade that was in my dream, that had to be Head Chef Grumbel," Tim said. Then, the fancy-handled sticker vanished as quickly as when its owner went through the windows. "We have to go find Link."

Todd, Tim, and Dink neatly folded up Granny's chairs, quietly left, and set out on their discovery mission.

Granny continued her seance and finally contacted Harvey. He told her of a communication that he had received from Chef Grumbel—it was mostly intended for the T&P members. The message also contained a recipe—expressly for Mrs. Hart—for *Glace de Viande* (meat jelly) that Mr. Grumbel had gained from his hero, the late, fabled French Chef, Auguste Escoffier. Mr. Grumbel had just taken a wonderful tour led by the culinary giant starting in the kitchen—the nerve center—of the Carlton, the grand hotel in London.

"Oh, boys, I have a telegram from *beyond* for you."

It was too late, the gang had already left the building.

Chapter 16

The atmosphere in Link's holding cell was turning warm, and the poop bag was adding an aroma similar to Limburger cheese inside the bizarre environment. He desperately hoped that his brother and the Tender twins would be wondering why he hadn't shown up at Granny's and come searching for their misplaced member.

Clank! Clank! Clank! PegLeg's stump was striking the polished cement floor of the room where Link was being held hostage.

Playlen could hear Coffery talking to his Nazi hound. "Don't worry, *Herr* Wolf, you'll be eating soon; some fresh, juicy meat." The dog began to yell uncontrollably.

Link, for a second time, heard the lock being released from its holder, and relief from the nails was forthcoming. Not only were there bloody pricks on his noggin, but now, as a result of his squirming, tiny tears in his skin had developed on his bare chest. But, the problem that advanced next was even worse. Coffery raised up the death lid and yanked Link from *horizontal* to 90-degree *vertical*. Right away, Link noticed something new about Deacon's uniform: he had a knife, with an ivory grip adorned with three gold-colored metal acorns, strapped to his right side...the blade was inside a black leather sheath that also had gold-tinted metal fittings. The cutter looked to be about a foot and a half.

"Do you like my German hunting knife? I keep it razor sharp using my grinding wheel. Here, I'll let you get a closer look." The tip of the small sword stopped just short of Link Playlen's right eyeball. PegLeg pushed his prisoner down and pulled him perpendicular; then, repeated the process.

"Hey, stay cool," Link said, trying to keep Coffery from discovering the real terror that he was feeling inside. "And tell that Gestapo mutt to shut up." After uttering that statement without thinking, he dearly hoped that he wasn't digging his hole deeper.

This time, after his involuntary sit-ups, he observed that the Nazi cur's collar was fixed to a chain that was attached to a stone wall. Sitting next to the chain was a metal wash tub with two identical handles.

Deacon Coffery left the room. When he returned, he was holding something behind his back. He brought it to the front of his disgusting, SS-looking body: a choice cut of bloody sirloin steak. PegLeg calmly hitched over to the excited canine and stuck the meat on the animal's nose; then, in a sissy underhand motion, tossed the NY strip toward Link's casket. The beef landed on a nail directly beside Link's belly. The raw meat began to drip blood slowly, and *Chinese Water Torture*, again, entered into Link's psyche.

The *Kommandant* returned to *Herr* Wolf's metal cord on the east wall, untangled it, and before young Playlen could think "bowwow," the bad-tempered pet had his hard claws scratching at the coffin, obsessed with retrieving his dinner. After indulging his darling dog, Coffery instructed him to *heil*. Deacon grabbed the steak and placed it in a dish adorned with black-red-and-yellow flags.

Pointed teeth flashed—devoured.

Coffery then double-backed to his human prey.

"I purchased some nice *Bratwurst* from my local butcher. The savory sausage is pan-frying in the kitchen. Also, six bottles of *Schultheiss* are chilling in the icebox. Would you care for some food and refreshment?" *Herr* Deacon asked. "*Schultheiss* is a hardy beer from Berlin for strong males like us, not like *Berliner Weiss*, which is low in alcohol and for weak men, women, and prissy children." After Link had pushed Principal Coffery to the limit in the swatting episode at Lakeside, PegLeg had gained a measure of respect for the durable kid. Unfortunately, as far as

Kommandant Coffery was concerned, this twin's fate was cast the moment he was born to Golda Playlen.

"How about some Pike and Plum Brandy, *Kommandant?* Do you have any available?" Link said. That was one of Golda's best meals to prepare, and Link and Dink were sometimes allowed a little sip of the *Pejsachowka* to go with the freshwater fish.

Playlen refused the offer for the German chow and booze. Maybe a bad choice.

Coffery seemed very disturbed that Link turned away his invitation to dinner. The *Kommandant* left the torture chamber in disgust.

He came back and was holding a large navy blue box with a phrase in white letters printed on the cover: "When It Rains It Pours." It also contained a very prominent yellow star with six, not five points like the gold ones the kids in Miss Tester's class would receive for each full week of attendance without an illness.

"I keep this in the cupboard for special situations such as yours," Coffery said. Deacon showed Link the easy-opening spout just before pouring the white crystals on young Playlen's open wounds.

"AAAAHHHH..." A moment later, the VP could barely hear Coffery.

"If he doesn't want to accept my grant of kindness, he can simmer-down with salt in his sores."

"*Heil*, Hitler!" The ear-piercing voice that responded to the *Kommandant's* statement belonged to Miss Eve Brown, Deacon's devoted assistant—there was no doubt in Link's fuzzy mind. As he was drifting into blackout, Playlen's last thoughts were:

Now I lay me down to sleep...if I shouuu...

Chapter 17

The three boys were each pushing their pedals at a furious pace toward Principal Coffery's, almost the entire time searching over their shoulders, hoping not to again cross paths with the spiritual typhoon that invaded Granny Hart's parlor.

"**Where could Link be?**" Dink yelled so his friends could hear him as they rode.

"**Don't worry, we'll find him**," Tim screamed back.

When they arrived at PegLeg's place, all the lights were off. The trio of T&P members walked timidly in the direction of the evil-looking door, and Dink reached inside the black wreath and grabbed the cold knocker.

Bang! Bang! Bang!—no answer. **Boom! Boom! Boom!** each kid hit the portal with a clenched fist trying to arouse someone, anyone, to get a response. The noise sounded as if it had filtered through the entry into a deep cavern.

Dink, despite feeling somewhat intimidated, was getting impatient. "Look at the trees," he said pointing to the Maples, "Link was here.

"**Is there anybody in there?**" Playlen yelled. "**We're looking for Link Playlen.**"

After five minutes of emptiness, a dog started to howl—an unsettling howl—but no humans came to the rescue. Todd decided: "It's useless to stand here any longer; I say we go to the cop shop." The idea was originally protested by the remaining duo, but the president eventually convinced them. They really had no other choice: none of their parents were home; Kim was still observing *Shiva* with the Steinbergs; Rod, Densel, and Warren were fulfilling the Halloween-cruising-for-chicks ritual; and Miss Tester was out of town.

The kids hopped back on their bikes and pumped toward downtown, where the *Bourbon kings*, Sheriff John Daniels and Deputy Jack Walker, were located.

Chapter 18

"Pour me some more of that Beam, will ya' Jack?" Sheriff John Daniels ordered.

"Okay, okay, be patient," Deputy Jack Walker responded as he tipped the booze bottle toward Daniels's glass, "one shot of *Jimmy* comin' up. You want a Budweiser to wash it down?"

"Yeah, sure," the sheriff grabbed the beer, "touch your Bud on mine. We finally caught us a ticket to the *big time*. Old lady Grumbel's neck is gonna stretch."

"Here's to us gettin' away from this dump and hittin' the *big time* as FBI agents in New York City."

"Yea, then we can a bag-a-biggie, like when Hoover's boys tagged Dillinger in Chicago back in Thirty-four." He formed a pretend gun with his right thumb and forefinger. "Go back and check on our *public-enemy-number-one,* Jack," Sheriff Daniels commanded.

"The old biddy is sleepin' and mumblin' somethin' 'bout gettin' even with some teenagers." As the deputy was walking back, he observed some movement on the street. He moved closer to one of the barred windows. "Looks like a nasty wind is kickin' up out there, no wonder my shoulder's actin' up," he said with a puzzled expression on his face. "I thought the weatherman said it was gonna be calm today."

As he approached the window, the "Wolf Man," the "Mummy," and "Count Dracula" suddenly popped up on the other side startling the second-fiddle. It was actually Dink, Tim, and Todd, minus Link.

All four wings of the T&P club, as well as the rest of the townsfolk, knew the story about John Daniels's shooting of Jack

Walker. It happened when the two law dogs were hunting deer while on vacation in upstate Pennsylvania in a little borough named Troy—nobody in St. Petersburg even noted that they were gone. Tim advised me (the Red Sox addict and communicator of the story that you, the reader, is presently reading) that according to Sheriff Daniels's telling, which was never denied by Deputy Walker, the unfortunate incident unfolded in this manner (the cop's tale revised for closer veracity by Tim):

The two peace officers enjoyed a breakfast of "ham and cheese omelettes," "home fries with grilled onions," and gallons of hardy "coffee" (thinned by shots of Wild Turkey— that fact left out by Daniels but confirmed by the owners of the restaurant, personal friends of the Tender clan) expertly prepared by the staff at the Edgewood Family Café—the finest eating establishment in Pennsylvania. Then, they set off with their rifles like real men to maim some innocent dear. The foamy head honcho said that he and Jack each had on camouflage suits bedecked with orange vests, so they could avoid accidentally killing each other. Daniels said they walked side-by-side deep into the woods, guns pointed forward in anticipation of animal annihilation. The pair was stalking near the valley of Mt. Pisgah when Walker spotted a doe—a female deer—mesmerized by a drop of golden sun that was shining directly into its wide, beautiful eyes. The deer apparently heard dried leaves crackling where the great white hunters were tramping, and the creature darted farther into the brush. Daniels recounted that he and Walker were so excited they almost urinated in their pants. The deputy lunged out in front to try and get the first shot off, but the sheriff tripped over a pair of rabbits, one under each leg, that had rushed into his path...his gun went off and a metal missile hit Deputy Jack in the left shoulder. John was so incensed, he immediately turned and fired at the twin hares but missed by a mile. He then focused his attention on Walker and finally decided that he better get him to the ER in Troy. Luckily, the injury wasn't too serious...a minor bleeder...and the doctor on duty retrieved the bullet. The deputy has kept the slug in his right pocket as a souvenir and a reminder, along with his left shoulder, never to track unsuspecting mammals again; especially, with Sheriff John Daniels.

The incident was big news in the small town, and Daniels and Walker made the front page of the Troy Gazette, the hamlet's local newspaper. A copy was mailed, mysteriously, to the Tender's home. The headline read:

OUT-OF-TOWN LAW OFFICERS FOILED BY "BEASTS OF THE WILD"

—rabbits, deer, and Turkey—
Deputy shot in shoulder by Sheriff.

Tim Tender could never understand how any human could shoot a defenseless animal, especially a heavenly one like a doe or a buck. But, Tim and Todd's dad, who hailed from Towanda, Pa., which was, ironically, located about fifteen miles east of Troy, told his twin sons that if hunters didn't hunt deer in the Pennsylvania woods, the state would be overrun with them. Also, without the million-plus *licenses to kill* sold yearly, the state's economy would suffer tremendously.

Tim didn't really buy it; but, after the explanation could understand some of the reasons for the ritual: for food to sustain other life or, maybe even, the motives that his father had mentioned.

What he couldn't or never would understand, was the objective that placed the animals' heads on the walls of countless dens in the homes of the courageous stalkers. This process done so that it can be proven to their friends and colleagues that *they* possess the tremendous skills needed to bravely track down and slay an unprotected four-legged beast of beauty.

Tim decided that he, too, would shoot animals; then, enjoy their beauty and magnificence through the reproduction process that his Polaroid "instant" camera afforded him. And, even though the pictures were only black and white, not showing all the wonderful colors, he would cherish the photos and the memories that they provided.

Bang! Bang! Bang! three separate knocks on the log-style door of the single-cell jailhouse brought Jack Walker to the front of the room.

"Ditch the liquor." Sheriff Daniels shoved the bottle of Jim Beam into the desk drawer and dropped his Bud into the wastebasket.

Deputy Walker did the same with his beer and shot, then opened the wooden portal. "Hey, you kids skedaddle, we don't have any candy." The kids ignored him and walked straight into the war room of the lockup. Dust from the street blew in behind them.

"We can't find my brother!" Dink said in a frantic tone.

"Maybe he doesn't want you to find him. Where's he supposed to be?" John queried.

"He was going to Principal Coffery's house to trick-or-treat and then was supposed to meet us at Granny Hart's," Todd said, "but he never showed up."

"What were you boys doin' at that old loon's place?" the under-sheriff questioned.

"Does it make any difference where we were?" Tim said. "Link is missing and we want to locate him."

"I'm sorry, boys, but an individual isn't considered missing until after twenty-four hours of being gone," John said aiming his thumb at the door. "We're not able to help you; come back in two days because we won't be here tomorr..."

"I was under the impression that it was less than twenty-four hours if the person is under the age of eighteen," Tim added. A confident look was starting to appear on his face.

"Think you're pretty smart, don't you kid?" Daniels said.

"Look, Sheriff Daniels told you punks to go aw..."

A couple of seconds before the last word completely came out of the deputy's mouth, the wooden door flew open and something resembling a cyclone came through. The two law dogs were picked up and violently thrown across the room; the three young boys ran for cover. Arrest-procedures papers, coffee-stained cups, fetters and handcuffs, revolver holsters, and FBI posters sailed everywhere.

After all the stormy action was complete, Tim was the first person to see that the cell door in the holding section was wide open. "Mrs. Grumbel is gone, she's gone!"

The rest of the mammoth wind's victims struggled up. The cops rushed to the cell.

"Great, we've lost our ticket outa here," Jack Walker said clutching the bars like a prisoner. "What the shit was that?"

"Hey! did my brother, Stinky, teach you that curse word, deputy?" Dink asked. "It's a good one, isn't it?"

"We think it was Head Chef Grumbel," Todd offered. "The same thing invaded Granny Hart's parlor."

"Isn't Chef Grumbel the old guy that almost killed the kid at Lakeside some years back with some tainted pork?" John said, as he pushed the cell door shut.

"Yea, Principal Coffery said he had had a private interview with the girl about her becomin' the captain of the new baton twirlin' team. Said it was a dream of hers; the name was Trudy Goldbat," the deputy said.

"Judy Goldberg, her name was Jud...you id..." Tim didn't finish what he really wanted to say.

"Right, Deacon told us she became really sick after eating her lunch at the meeting, and if not for the nurse making an untimely entrance into his office, Trudy might have died," Daniels added.

"Judy, you mor..." Todd put his palms over his mouth to stop himself from getting into trouble.

"Yea, Mr. Coffery fired Chef Grumbel for preparin' undercooked pork," Deputy Walker said.

"Head Chef Grumbel got a raw deal!" Tim yelled. "He was ill that day and wasn't even working; besides, you guys never even tested the pork dish, just let PegLeg throw it out in the trash."

"Well, he was concerned that none of the other kids eat the meal by mistake," the sheriff motioned everyone to the front of the office, "even said he had sacrificed his own lunch to help Trudy fulfill her goal. And! referring to your principal as 'PegLeg' is disrespectful."

"Anyway," the deputy said, "that Grumbel dude is dead. Are you tryin' to tell us that there's some supernatural crap goin' on?"

"That's it, it's his spirit, his ghost, his wayward soul, whatever you want to call it," Tim said. "We think you had the wrong Grumbel in your jail cell, and you guys upset her husband."

"What the hell you talkin' 'bout ghosts and spirits and that kinda crap," Deputy Walker said, "maybe you kids been drinkin' some other kind of spirits that's causin' you to tell such wacko stories."

"Hey Walker, you and Stinky must've attended the same Dale Carnegie class for *Effective Swearing*, you know all the words," Dink returned. "I'm trying to quit my cursing but it's difficult. Link told me it would get me in trouble some day."

Todd jumped into the conversation. "Look, man, we're too young to drink firewater. Besides, between you and Daniels, this place has become a dry county," he pointed at the desk, "we saw you push that bottle into the drawer."

"Mr. Grumbel's ghost has visited each one of us in different places; we think he's responsible for the deaths of Carl Steinberg and Eddie Liebowitz and maybe the Barren clan," Tim said, "I mean look at facts, only the facts, huh?" He placed his hands on the sheriff's desk as if he was standing at a podium.

"Head Custodian Grumbel lost her husband—and her right thumb and forefinger—in an automobile accident on Twenty-fifth Street.

"Now, Mr. Daniels and Mr. Walker, see if you can follow me on this...the two Barren kids were both missing the thumbs and index fingers off their right hands. This was also the case with the Liebowitz boy. And, finally, Cookie's right finger was severed completely and his thumb was dangling where something—not a reptile—tried to cut it off. Are you beginning to see a connection?"

"Don't you mean disconnection?" Walker said, trying to hold back a chuckle.

"That's good, Jack," Daniels responded, also smiling.

"Please, don't interrupt, man," Todd aimed a finger at his brother, "continue Tim."

"Thanks. We, the members of the outstanding T&P club, believe that though Mrs. Grumbel has become a nasty person—some even call her a witch—she's not capable of such acts. But, a ghost with vengeance on his mind, or whatever he has up top, may be capable of anything. Nobody knows but the ghost, other ghosts, or people like Granny Hart, huh? Look, Todd saw the spirit of Chef Grumbel standing over Eddie, and Dink sighted it hovering over dead Cookie—in both cases carrying a large kitchen knife. We also think that the wind that just blew in here broke his wife out and may have kidnapped Link. So, can we please go find Link, huh?"

"Sorry, boys, but our law is the law, and young Playlen hasn't been missing long enough for us; besides, isn't that quite a tall tale?" Sheriff John said. "We don't believe in ghosts, and our ex-prisoner, arrested for some of the reasons you just mentioned, escaped after the twister—one of nature's own—broke the lock and burst open the cell door." He stood up abruptly.

Obviously, Tim's sublime speech entered the top law dog's ear on one side of his head; flowed through the alcohol in his brain; and came out drunk on the other side. The bottom law dog wasn't even worth wasting time on to persuade—the ultimate "yes" man.

The "Mummy," with "Count Dracula" and the "Wolf Man" directly behind, pushed open the log door. They all left disgusted but not surprised.

"Release *Jimmy* and pour me another shot, will ya," Walker pleaded.

"Yea, we'll track down our killer in due time," Daniels returned. "Tap my glass. Later on we'd better go over to old lady Hart's house and see what she knows, if anything."

Chapter 19

Link Playlen could sense something heavy and slimy crawling up from his right foot onto the Army pants covering his legs. As well as removing Link's shirt, Coffery had taken off his red Keds. Link felt his face, no sweat, but he started to think an unnatural act was about to take place.

The last thing he remembered before he had passed out was the terrible pain that the salt oozing into his wounds brought forth; but, now for some reason, there was no agony at all. Was this a dream? He didn't know; it had the feel of real, too real.

And, what ungodly creature was casually making its way up his not-yet-teenaged body? Maybe he wouldn't even make his teen years—the years during which he was supposed to have the best times of his life?

Suddenly, he realized that a second heavy and slimy being was moving inch-by-inch up his other leg, trying to catch number one. Slowly, slowly, slowly—the thing took longer to advance—Link thought—than the span it will take some slugger to break the "Bambino's" single season record set in 1927 of 60 *four-baggers*. For some reason, the number thirty-four entered his brain. The thought faded.

The original crawler stopped and waited patiently for its leader. They seemed to be enjoying the pace and, after what felt like years, turned and stared at each other. They actually had mugs on their lengthy whatever's.

They reversed back to their original direction and lunged toward Playlen's chest—the faces were now visible.

"PegLeg? What th..." Link blurted. On the right was Deacon Coffery, face as red as a four-hour sunburn.

The one on the left had a plain-looking front—a wide nose with a small, square, dark moustache running only the width of the bottom part of its snout. Its short hair was parted on the right, pushed over, and matted down to the left. But, the most mesmerizing section of its kisser was the eyes, black eyes that could hypnotize a soul.

"I know that face from somewhere."

Principal Coffery's head began to take shape with *Kommandant* Coffery's SS hat on its top and spoke to the left headache, "Long live the Third Reich."

"Heil! Hitler," the *other* returned.

Suddenly, both of the monsters' mouths opened—each containing teeth in the shape of daggers—*chomp! chomp! chomp!*—the beasts now moving with the speed of an *Indy* car toward Link's own head—each splitting young Playlen's face in half with the skill of a surgeon using a scalpel...blood spurted everywhere inside the death box.

Link woke up and touched his face—there were no gaping holes, there was no blood. But, now there was plenty of sweat. It had only been a dream...a nightmare...an hallucination, and he was still alive. "Hal-l-l...lelujah!"

Playlen began to hear loud talking, so he listened carefully to determine its origination. The high-volume chatting soon became screaming at the end of each line spoken, then the whole process repeated over and over. He realized that the tirade was coming from Coffery's phonograph, and the person was speaking in a language other than English, he sensed German. The yelling finally and mercifully ended.

The coffin lid opened—*Kommandant* Coffery obviously decided to disperse with the niceties this time because he didn't even *rap, rap, rap* on the casket door. This time he wasn't dressed in his SS regulars. He had on, instead, a light grey three-piece suit with the jacket open and the bottom button on the vest unbuttoned; shiny, dark grey shoes; and a grey fedora with a black silk band surrounding the hat.

"Playlen, do you like my new suit?" Deacon said prancing like a gimpy model. "I bought it to wear on the job. You can call me 'Mr. Suit.' Did you enjoy the wonderful sermon that I played you?"

"Who was that guy, what kind of *shpil* was that?" Link returned. "He sounded really mad." Playlen thought he better engage in Coffery's delusion to keep him from seasoning Link's body again with the white stuff.

"It was the pilot of my party; he left us in 1945, far too soon. In fact, my guide and his wife died tragically on the same day, just one day after they married...a truly sad story. But his devoted followers, like myself, will continue to bring his message to the world...his ideals will live on." Coffery then stood at attention. **"WE WILL HAVE OUR *LEBENSRAUM*, *MY* PEOPLE ARE AGAIN ON THE MARCH! THE *UNTERMENSCHEN* WILL BE NO LONGER!!"**

"You're hurting my ears, pipe down and tell me more...what's *Lebens*...? What's *Unter*...? I don't understand."

"My life is education, and I will attempt to teach you a serious lesson...maybe you can be my *Kapos*, another trustee in the struggle to carry my people back to the forefront of the universe, where we belong. You're not pure bred—where I worked in the war, some of your mother's kind helped the cause against their *own* to avoid pain and suffering, the great persuaders."

"What plans do you have for me?" Link asked with trepidation.

"I know you're a strong kid," Principal Coffery took off his jacket and made a muscle with his right bicep, "but I must be sure that you can survive under extreme situations; so, experiments are forthcoming."

"What are you talking about? What kind of experiments? More Morton's?"

"Oh, that, that was just retaliation for refusing my invitation to a dinner that I had slaved over for hours."

"Then...what?"

"All in due time, all in due time, young Playlen," Coffery beamed. "If you survive the tests, maybe you can lead my youth movement. Such a distinction should make you proud."

Proud was not the word Link Playlen would have used. But, he was still impersonating, "Did I hear you talking with Miss Brown earlier? Is she helping your cause?"

"Eve Brown is my first *aide-de-camp*, as a matter of fact, she's going on her initial assignment to see if she can make the grade. She'll be reasoning with a pesky individual in a close-by neighborhood."

Just then, Miss Brown walked in dressed in a brown vest over a white blouse, blue skirt, and heavy-looking shoes and socks. Her normally swollen hair was pushed down and pulled back. She raised her right arm to the Nazi symbol on the ceiling, said, "*Heil* to the Leader," and left abruptly without saying a word to Link.

"What neighbor?" Link said.

"Just someone who called while you were sleeping and threatened me," Deacon returned. "We can't let that sort of thing fester." He moved his forefinger across his neck.

"'**While you were sleeping**?' You anus, you caused me to pass out."

"**What!** did you call me?" Coffery banged the coffin.

"Cool it, I just said, said you, you...you genius, you came up with an inventive method to give me some shuteye," Link said, remembering that he needed to keep the *Kommandant* off-guard. "What did the neighbor try to intimidate you with?"

"Oh, you don't need to concern yourself with that now. Maybe I'll fill you in later, when I know you can be trusted. It's too bad your brother, Dink, can't be here. It would make the examinations move along much faster. Do you know the variety of pig known as the *guinea*?"

Chapter 20

"Let's stop at the Wheelhouse Bar and Grille before headin'
over to old lady Hart's," Deputy Walker requested. "I could go
for one of them tasty cheeseburgers; besides," he said as his tongue
met his upper lip, "I need another shot of Jim Beam after goin'
'bottoms-up' with that bottle in the squad car."

"Sure, why not; I need a bite to eat and a shot, too," Sheriff
Daniels said, "but I'll also have to have a Bud chaser to wash it all
down." He held three fingers up. "Who needs the three R's when
you got the three B's—bourbon, burgers, and beer."

* * *

Knock! Knock! Knock! **Trick-or-Treat**."

"Who's out there, is it Roddy?" Granny said as she walked
toward the front door. "Oh, wonderful, I have plenty of treats left,
you know. Just a moment while I unlock my locks." She opened
the door. "That's a beautiful crimson cape and matching hood
you're wearing. And your long red gloves are elegant—such a
nice costume. Who are you supposed to be, anyway? Here, have
some candy."

"Screw the candy, you old bag," the caped person said, and
with the force of a cannon shot elbowed Granny back into the
foyer.

The plastic pumpkin fell to the ground. Chocolate-covered
beetles seemed to crawl out of the orange and black container
that came to rest on Mrs. Hart's body.

* * *

"I guess we better get goin'," Jack Walker said, "last call's over."

"Sure, but let's get a *b & b* for the road," John Daniels said signaling the bartender. "If the barkeep refuses, we'll pull the joint's liquor license. You better drive; I've had too much."

"What'ya mean?" Walker put a thumb up. "You had one less than me. We should lock up the squad car and call a cab."

* * *

The cabby dropped the two lawmen off at the curb in front of Granny's and said he'd be back after his next fare. Daniels and Walker climbed and stumbled up the steep slope to the front door, and the deputy managed a meek knock. Nobody answered.

"Hit the door harder," the sheriff ordered.

Jack reached back with both hands, smacked the thick wooden portal, and fell head-first into the front hallway— the door was already open. John Daniels staggered in, tried to rescue his second-in-command, but also ended up belly- down on the floor. The interior of the house was completely dark. They eventually managed to make their way into the kitchen, where they noticed bowls of food on the table....The deputy decided that he was still hungry and started to eat the leftover vittles.

"This grub has a nice crunch," Walker commented as he chewed the pest-filled pasta, "have some."

"Forget it." Daniels told Walker to put down the food. "Let's check upstairs."

The two bozos next found themselves in the master bedroom on the second floor, and must have thought that they were in the warm confines of their own homes: each dunce jumped into the bed. In the process, a body—or something— was knocked to the hardwood.

"Crap!" the deputy said as he jumped up from the bed, "what was that?"

"I don't know, but now it's nothing but a huge pile of dust. Let's get outa here."

The two local lawmen rushed out of the bedroom toward the stairs like Keystone Cops. They tripped over each other; rolled head over heels down to the first floor; and slammed their bourbon-and-beer-soaked noggins on the floorboard. They were each knocked out.

The driver of the yellow *limo* pulled up to the mansion on Demens Drive and walked up to the front door, which was wide open. "Is there anybody in here? Sheriff Daniels, Deputy Walker, are you here?" He managed to find the light switch in the hallway, flicked it on, and immediately observed two bodies spread-eagle on the deck. "Sheriff Walker and Deputy Daniels? Huh?" The driver retrieved some water from the first floor toilet—where something brown and large first had to be removed from the bowl—and splashed the liquid on the officers' faces. The cop duo came around.

The trio moved into the front parlor.

Daniels lit—no easy task in his condition—his *J. Edgar Hoover* lighter in an effort to find a light switch for the chandelier. "Walker! Why are you wearing my uniform?"

"I don't know! Why are you wearin' my uniform?" Walker said with amazement.

"Hey! fellas, does it matter?" the cabby said pointing toward the rug. "Can't you see the body in the wedding dress?"

The body belonged to Granny Hart; she was lying on the rug belly-up and dead. With non-darkness now spread over the area, a few other abnormal things became evident.

There was a pool of blood next to Mrs. Hart's head.

"Walker, turn the body over," Daniels commanded.

"Nice hair," the deputy said sarcastically as he pushed aside Granny's dirty gray locks—now sticky from the dark red blood, "there's a small hole in the back of her neck."

"Check out her hands," the cab driver added.

Granny's hands were bound together at the wrist with chicken wire. There was blood trickling from the wounds caused by the steel wire.

"Who...whoa! Look over the fireplace. What the...is that?" The sheriff moved closer to the mantel.

"What is that supposed to mean?" Deputy Walker asked with a baffled look on his face.

"Beats me," the cabby said.

"Who asked you?" Daniels said, staring in the cab driver's direction, "get outa here, we'll take care of this."

"How're you two going to get to the station house?"

"Oh," John said, "right, right; you can stick around, just don't touch anything."

"That's right, cabby," Walker added as he retrieved, barehanded, from the floor, the broken frame of Granny and Harvey Hart's wedding picture, "we don't want the crime scene to be corrupted."

The wall over the facing of the fireplace was painted a deep black color...on top of the paint was the number "11"...directly opposite, on the bottom, the number "10."

* * *

Later, the coroner wrote in his post-mortem paper that Mrs. Hart was indeed killed by the wound in her neck. He continued in the report that the single bullet came from a small-caliber firearm. The type of gun had yet to be ascertained; although, he speculated that it was not made in America.

An additional fact authored by the M.E.—entirely missed at the scene by the cop bunglers: Granny's body was minus its right thumb, right forefinger, and two front gold crowns.

Chapter 21

The Monday After Halloween

Dink Playlen was mystified by the note that was taped to his school locker:

I'm back from Three Egg. Please meet me behind the Lakeside cafeteria as soon as you read this. I'll be waiting.

Forever yours, Lorraine

Dink Playlen was supposed to meet Tim and Todd in the library an hour before classes started, so that they could track down a book dealing with the subject of *ghost hunting*.

The trio felt very sad about Granny's demise but had to locate their missing member. Besides, Todd had eased their emotions when he said with compassion, "Mrs. Hart is now with Mr. Hart and can talk to him see-through-face to see-through-face."

Granny's lawyer had found her will, not an easy task. Mrs. Hart's wish was to be cremated, and no one was to make a fuss over funeral arrangements. Her ashes were to be scattered in Tampa Bay just outside her beloved "den of the departed." A. Hister reassured everyone that he would take care of the dispersal.

Instead of uniting with the Tender twins, Dink decided to follow his *heart*, "I have to go to Lorraine"; then, he headed for the cafeteria. When he reached the rear of the lunchroom, he hunted for Lorraine but failed to find her. He continued his pursuit farther out by the garbage can area, thinking, just for a moment, how bad the stench was near the dumping grounds. "Lorraine! Lorraine! Where are you?"

In the following instant, a wet cloth was forcibly placed over Dink's nose and mouth. He struggled but shortly thereafter became one with his dreams.

* * *

After retrieving some valuable information and waiting thirty minutes for Dink, Todd and Tim went to locate him. Luck was not their friend that morning, and they were forced to visit the principal's headquarters. When they entered the outer office, one-half of the T&P club found that Miss Brown wasn't behind her desk. Principal Coffery came out of his inner suite wearing a grey suit and holding a grey hat.

"What can I do for the Tender twins this bright morn...?" Deacon Coffery inhaled, began to sneeze, grabbed for the kerchief in the top pocket of his coat, felt emptiness, and exhaled slime into his hand. After disposing of the nasty substance on Miss Brown's desk, he turned back toward the Tenders.

Tim noticed something out-of-the-ordinary about Coffery's outfit. "Did you know that there's a stain above your breast pocket?"

"Uh...ye...yes, I spilled some...some coffee," Coffery said in disgust, "and this is a brand new suit. So, for the second time, what do you two want?" He was becoming impatient.

"Man, have you seen Dink?" Todd said. "He was supposed to have met us in the library forty-five minutes ago."

"No, I haven't come in contact with Dink Playlen or his brother Link. Now, if there's nothing else, I have some important matters to attend to."

"By the way, where is Miss Brown today?" Tim asked.

"She called in sick. This office will be closed the rest of the day." PegLeg Coffery shuffled the boys out of the room, limped down the hallway, and disappeared beyond the door of the fifth-grade classroom.

"I wish Miss Tester was here; she would know what to do," Tim said. "It was kind of curious that Coffery mentioned Link when we didn't even ask about him, huh?"

"Man, brother, you're right; by the way, when is Miss Tester going to return?"

"Later this week, tomorrow I think."

Miss Tester had been in Helen, Georgia, since before the start of the present school year. She was helping with a very ill relative and was due back in Saint Petersburg, Tuesday, the second day of November.

The Lakeside bell rang. The Tender twins had to go to Mrs. Long's class. As they entered the room, there were two empty seats: the desks usually occupied by their best friends.

* * *

"*Fraulein* Brown, have you prepared the second coffin for the second twin?" *Kommandant* Coffery questioned.

"*Ja, Herr* Coffery, everything is as you ordered," Eve Brown said as she completed a "*heil*-Hitler" sign. "The young Jews are in their place."

"Wonderful, your training is progressing beautifully. *Der Fuehrer* will be proud of you."

"It is my duty to serve him. How are the funds for our major project?"

"With the assets that you recently brought in, and after the rate of exchange, we're only 756 *Reichmarks* short of the 133,756 needed for the oven."

"And now we have a couple of strong, young boys to handle the labor," the secretary said.

"I have some red wine*,* " *the kommandant* said as he was corkscrewing a green bottle*,* "a nice bottle of *Bordeaux* that I secured in France—vintage, November of '42. Let us celebrate our newest patient. The rewards of research will soon begin."

Chapter 22

Erik and Golda Playlen could not find either of their identical twins. Warren, along with Rod and Densel, didn't have any luck either. The remaining members of the Tender family, including baby Everett but not Kim, also met a dead-end. Kim was still at *Shiva* and couldn't take phone calls. The *lost boys* were being seeked *every which way but loose* but could not be found. That Monday night, there wouldn't be any sleep in the Playlen household and little— not joyful—in the Tenders' home.

* * *

Dink Playlen was furiously pedaling his bike westward on First Avenue North, trying to get to Twenty-fifth Street, so he could then head south toward Twenty-second Avenue and west again to Auburn Street, the shut-off road that he lived on. He had just bought the newest *Superman* comic book from the wonderful Haslam's Bookstore on Central Avenue and Twentieth Street— reputed to be the largest bookshop in the state of Florida. He wanted desperately to get home and read the comic.

"Move your legs, boy," Dink said to himself. His lower limbs picked up the pace.

Everything around him was white, an extremely intense white. Plus his clothes, his Schwinn, even Superman's outfit on the cover was white.

Then, a tremendous feeling of urgency came over Dink and he pulled off the road into the lot of an abandoned bank....He ripped open the bag that held his superhero purchase and began to read with a rage.

Suddenly, he looked up; he saw nothing. Dink looked back down at his reading material and continued through the pages. Something, again, drew his head upward, but this time his eyes focused squarely on the head of a black cat, its own eyes as white as the white in the rest of the surroundings. Dink also noticed blood, lots of rich red blood on the cat's whiskers.

"What th...?"

Before Playlen could say *Meow*, the feline—with its body minus the head—leapt onto Dink's face and scratched it with needle-like claws. The headless frame opened deep gashes but, strangely, no blood flowed. Young Dink glanced up toward the roof one more time, and the treacherous tom's mouth was grinning, a big grin.

Dink woke up. "Finally, that's over. Hallelujah!"

He was in Coffery's coffin, built especially for him...identical to his twin brother's. He was gazing up at the nails that were just six inches above his body. Then the nails turned to syringes; just as quickly, the syringes became straight needles like the kind his mother used to stitch his torn pants after a hard day at the playing office. Nails, old hypodermics, and rusty knitting pins flashed in front of his peepers, never wavering the sequence. Each time a different form of sharpness appeared, it stretched downward, down until the points of the small metal rods pierced the skin over Playlen's entire body. They even punctured through his pants, which was the only article of clothing, like his sibling, that Coffery let him keep on. The steel spikes pushed directly through him—continuing to switch shapes—and into the bottom of the casket.

Blood spurted out of newly-formed body cavities like a volcano erupting its lava. Blood flooded down Dink's chin, down his neck, down his chest, down his belly, down his legs, up and over his feet, and ended in a crimson puddle. The pond then began to levitate...the blood kept rising and rising like a red geyser stuck in slow motion, until it completely covered every inch of Dink Playlen except his face. It suddenly halted as if it had to take a rest from its constant pressing. An hour passed on, or so it seemed, an additional hour...nothing.

Then, like *Montezuma's revenge*, the scarlet liquid flowed once again. He wanted to curse—he wouldn't. The vital fluid of life moved up his face and stopped just below his eyes.

The coffin lid flew back as quickly as a swallow's flight of migration. There stood—not Coffery or Eve—but the Vault-Keeper from Tim's *The Vault of Horror* comics with his green hood covering his long, stringy gray hair and silhouetting his ugly mug and boil-dotted chin. He was holding a bucket of blood and threw it on Dink's eyes, completing the *drowning pool*.

Dink woke up, again.

"Was it a bad dream within a bad dream? Yes! Oh sh—! No, I won't say it, not even think it anymore. I'm swearing off swearing.

"I'm sweating like a...no, don't say it. I'm alive!"

Now, would the real horror begin?

Chapter 23

The Tuesday Morning After Halloween

"Tim, wake up, shake a leg; we're going to be late for the search," Mom Tender said. School has been cancelled today so as many people as possible can be congregated to look for Link and Dink. We have to go by the Steinberg's and get your sister, then meet your father, Todd, and Rod in the parking lot at Webb's City. After that, we have to catch up with everyone else gathering at Williams Park."

Williams Park was located downtown in the heart of the city, where many special events such as celebrations and concerts and conversations occurred. It was a wonderful place: four acres of honored ground as notable and enjoyable as the community's famed beaches.

Tim, known for his dreams, nightmares, sleeping fantasies, was wishing that the disappearance of his two best friends could be an illusion instead of the real situation that it had become. He sat up, then got up, and the first thing he saw was his Peter Lorre poster and those bug-eyes that seemed to be watching his every move. "What are you looking at?"

He dressed quickly, ran outside, and jumped into his mother's 1952 Ford Fairlane. Dad Tender had already left with Todd and Rod in the most popular demonstrator of 1954. "Do you think Kim is feeling better, Ma?"

"I hope so; we couldn't contact her during *Shiva*."

"Why?" Tim shifted in the front seat.

"It's a Jewish custom in the death of a loved one and we want to honor that."

"I agree." A smile came on young Tender's face.

"Your sister is a strong person; I'm sure she'll be fine."

The Steinbergs lived in the Roser Park section of town near Mound Park Hospital, a healing and delivery place where a hefty number of St. Petersburg citizens had entered the world. The entire Roser Park area was unique because it actually had hills, maybe the only ones in the state of Florida. The roads were all made of red, not pink, brick. The streets wound down and up and around a waterway that contained sewers to dump the rain from off the top of Ninth Street, and other thoroughfares. This situation provided the T&P gang with one of the most fun things that they spent their leisure time doing: crawling up the sewer pipes and finishing at eye-level to the street where all the automobiles were zooming by. Also, pedestrians would foot their way down Ninth toward their destinations, and the kids, when they were collectively in a mischievous frame of mind, would call out to the weary walkers. Then the boys would watch as the clueless ones tried to figure out where the sounds were originating from.

Of course, the risk involved—which actually made it more thrilling—was the ever-present possibility that an out-of-nowhere Florida thunderstorm would surface and flush dirt and leaves down the drains, over the boys, through the cement tunnels, and into the canals of Booker Creek.

* * *

After the whole Tender family assembled together at "The Most Unusual Drugstore," they caravaned to Williams Park and met the Playlens—minus Link and Dink—plus many of the prominent families, some who were descendants of the township's *founding fathers*:the Williamses, from the family tree of General John C. Williams, constructor of the city in 1888—at 27 degrees-45' north LATITUDE to 82 degrees-38' west LONGITUDE. The park was named after the General, and also, because he hailed from the Michigan city of Detroit, the first hotel was titled after his hometown; the Browns—no relation to Eve—were ancestors of Major Lew B. Brown, owner of the evening version of the day-time paper whose motto was: "Free paper for every day the Sun doesn't shine on our fair city." He was pretty safe with that claim because at some point during the day, old Mr. Sol usually showed his face in the community. The Major had originally brought his wife to town from Kentucky for health reasons; the Rosers, a division of the C. M. Roser clan from Ohio—*C. M.* was already a millionaire, partly from sales of the dear departed Carl Steinberg's favorite cookie, the Fig Newton; and the Pheils, owners of the Pheil Hotel and Movie Complex. The Pheils also had the distinction of being the family with the first set of twins born in Mound Park Hospital.

There were many other ancestries represented: the Straubs, the Belchers, the Disstons, the Demens—all at the common ground to help find the *lost boys*.

"Even Hattie, Ed, and Frank Boore are here," Todd mentioned to his twin.

"Yes, they cancelled their annual Hattie's Attic sale of an-tiques and great junk. They also put off the restaurant's yearly delivery of snow sent from Buffalo in exchange for Florida or-anges that fly to the North for the winter," Tim said, his hand portraying a plane taking off.

A. Hister was also available and told everyone that anyone who wanted to go with him in his huge black funeral car, could, providing their was enough room for their bodies. No one volun-teered.

"You know," Tim whispered to Todd, "it's a little odd that Coffery would cancel classes at school and then not show up for the search."

"Miss Brown," Todd returned as he pointed over the massive squad of searchers, "is absent, too."

And, the *Bourbon Kings* were "no shows"—it was rumored that Sheriff Daniels and Deputy Walker were still hunting for the alleged maniac maintenance monarch, Mrs. Glinda Grumbel.

"Let's get our bikes out of Dad's trunk and look on our own, Tim," Todd said.

"Sounds great." The twins moved in the direction of the car.

The rest of the Tenders, all the remaining Playlens, and the other compassionate citizens of the community split up and started to comb the city.

First, the Tender twins biked passed the south entrance of the Soreno Hotel, where the noble sculpture of the Griffin Birds surrounding the Soreno Knight guarded the building, toward Central Avenue. There, they talked to ex-tourists, now happy residents, that were sitting, sunning, and trying to relax on the famous "green benches" that lined the street on both sides—block after block after block. This day there seemed to be a sort of tension in the air.

A good portion of these transplants—most of them, in fact—were retirees. They had moved from former cities and former jobs all over the *U.S.A.*: steelworkers from Pittsburgh, autoworkers from Detroit, crabbers from Baltimore, brewery workers from St. Louis and Milwaukee, ex-gamblers from Las Vegas, cowboys from Dallas, and editors from New York City. And—many of them hailed from other countries before coming to America. They had all arrived in Florida for an easier way of life, one where their bodies could enjoy the wonderful weather of the "Sunshine City" and the "rays of health" that came down from the sky, nearly on a daily basis.

Only, right now, there was *A Fly in the Ointment, A Monkey in the Stillson Wrench*. Someone or some *thing* was interrupting the quiet nature of this once unmolested town. The boys hoped that somebody—anybody—could give them any information about their missing friends.

The Playlen twins, because of their duplicate looks remindful of the great actor, Ernest Borgnine, usually received a second glance, and Tim felt that someone must have seen them, or possibly have some idea where they were.

Chapter 24

"*Frau* Eve, it is time to wake the young Jews and show them our 'hall of fame,'" *Herr* Coffery said as he handed her two pair of handcuffs, "restrain them."

"*Ja*! *Kommandant*," the second-in-command returned. She cuffed the boys' hands behind their rear ends.

The Playlen twins were then led down a long hallway, where the floor was covered with a rug adorned with East German flags. They had just been brought out of a deep sleep and were still a little groggy, not to mention somewhat in pain.

Along the corridor on both sides of the wall was picture after picture of German soldiers, plus one of the LEADER. Link and Dink were introduced to each and given a short, deadly history lesson.

PegLeg Coffery began to speak about these people as if they were some kind of gods to be idolized:

"This first picture is Julius Streicher, an early member of the Nazi party. He published *Der Sturmer*, a wonderful periodical known for its enlightening material about anti-Semitism."

"A true compatriot," the *Frau* said. Her right hand and arm shot up toward the painting.

"Second in the lineup is Heinrich Himmler," Coffery pushed the boys farther down the hall, "a personal favorite of mine and one of the original members of the Nazi party. He was leader of the *Gestapo* from 1936 to 1945 and enforcer of the forced-labor and concentration camps," Coffery continued. "Also, he was the brilliant creator of the *Final Solution*."

"A true compatriot," Eve offered, as she performed the *heil-Hitler* sign again.

"Thirdly, Paul Joseph Goebbels, one of Hitler's first followers and 'propaganda' minister in 1933—artist of the 'large truth' that was mostly directed at the Jewish race. He was also the overseer of German radio, press, cinema, and theater."

"A true compatriot," *Frau* Eve said, as if she had a tape recorder in her mouth.

"Next, a person that I was privileged to be able to assist in his great work," *Herr* Deacon said, the excitement increasing in his voice, "the innovative Josef Mengele, the polite doctor of Auschwitz, known as the 'Angel of Death' because of his enthusiasm for selecting Jews for the gas chambers. He was also responsible for the famed twin experiments. I will be following many of his studies in working with the 'identicals,' when I allow you Playlens to become products of *my* research. I'm sure that you will feel exalted at this once-in-a-lifetime opportunity."

"**A true compatriot!**" the female puppet yelled.

"**Oh, shut your damn trap!**" Dink screamed, breaking his vow to himself not to curse. "You sound like a parrot." She was driving him crazy with the "true compatriot" babble.

"**Dink!** watch it, you may have done it now." Link scolded his twin.

"**Let me inflict pain on the insubordinate,** *Herr Kommandant!*" the Frau cried—her creepy voice filled with fury.

"All in good time, Eve, all in good time. We must continue the introductions." He was shoving the twins around so much that they began to feel like the balls in a pinball machine. "This next man I taught most of what he knows, although he would claim the opposite, about leadership and how to deal with one's enemies. Meet Rudolph Hoss, the SS Kommandant of Auschwitz, the one responsible, with my direction, for reducing prisoners to strolling skeletons, which is what subhumans should look like...fit only for death...an honorable end for such inferior people." The *kommandant* brought his left forefinger across his neck.

"And here we have Rudolf Hess, not to be confused with Hoss, who was named deputy chancellor in 1933 and in 1939 became second in succession to the Nazi throne."

Link whispered to Dink, "This guy isn't at all who we thought he was; he's some kind of wacked-out Nazi."

Dink responded under his breath, "Yea, and I think he's got her brainwashed."

"Stop jabbering!" *Herr* PegLeg snapped, "I'm trying to teach you about some of the great men of the past. Finally, a man who really needs no introduction, the author of Nazism; the author of the Third Reich; and the author of *Mein Kampf*, the greatest book of all eternity...about his struggle for a better world. Meet the LEADER, the one and only, Adolf Hitler. Quite moving, isn't he?"

Both Coffery and Eve *heiled* to Hitler's likeness.

The painting of just Hitler's head—colored in black, white, and red with his squatty moustache, wide nose, flattened-down hair parted from right to left, and evil eyes—looked lifelike. A situation that frightened the Playlen twins, but now stirred their courage; therefore, they let their true feelings come out. They couldn't help themselves.

"Right, he moves me right toward a bowel movement," Link said.

"Yea, and Link's usually full of crap, so it'll be nice and messy," Dink added without hesitation.

"**Frau Coffery, prepare the coffee!**" *Kommandant* Coffery yelled.

"Right away," *Herr* chief, "it will be my personal pleasure." Eve immediately left the hallway.

"You know, PegLeg, we learned about this German Army machine in one of Miss Tester's World History lessons," Dink said, not able to hide the disgust on his face.

"And what was cool about the lecture is that it taught us the truth about the idiots you have on your wall: they were tried for war crimes, unspeakable to decent people, and the freaks were either executed, got life imprison, or took the real courageous way out and killed themselves—like your so-called leader," Link said with conviction.

"Role models supreme," Dink added. *"Doc, Grumpy, Happy, Sleepy, Sneezy, Bashful,* and...and...damn, I can never get all of them. Link, who's the last one?"

"Dopey!...fits perfect with Adolf."

"Right, *Dopey*," Dink held up five fingers on one hand and two on the other, "the Seven Dwarfs have more guts than your freaks."

"**Frau!**" Coffery shouted toward the kitchen. "Is the coffee ready yet? Make sure it is scorching HOT."

"Nein, it is not quite there, but the dark, rich liquid will be steaming at its highest level momentarily. Can you hear the wonderful musical tones of the whistling?"

The pitch became ringing in the twins' ears, and the coffee...severe pain in the mouths of Dink and Link Playlen.

Dink was first.

"Did your mother ever wash your mouth out with soap, you little creep?" Eve said to Dink as she pushed a stein of steaming coffee toward him. "Here, try some of my special German-roast discipline and see how many cuss words come out of your filthy mouth."

The coffee was not sipped but force-chugged.

Link was next.

Eve patted herself on the back. *"Auf wiedersehen*, boys."

Chapter 25

Tim and Todd stopped in front of Denington's for a cold drink; Todd put a nickel in the royal blue Pepsi dispenser. Mr. Denington had put the machine in new, early 1952, so that his customers could get a soda when his store wasn't open. He was also trying to locate the Playlen twins. Todd downed half the soda in one gulp and passed the remainder to his brother; Tim drank his share as if he was testing a fine wine. After the refreshment, they were rejuvenated and started pedalling toward the Playlen home and its neighboring cemetery.

The boys approached the pink palace in Playlen land and screeched their bikes to a sudden halt. They each stared at a "For Sale" sign in the front yard—one from R. W. Caldwell, a real estate agency in Gulfport. Each twin froze and looked like one half of a Popsicle.

Todd broke the trances, "Man, do you see what I s...?"

"Yes! Where do you suppose they're going to move, huh?" Tim said—the look of disbelief still evident on his young face.

"Probably anywhere away from here; I guess they feel the town is getting too crazy," Todd returned.

"Isn't it, huh?"

"I don't understand what's happening? People are turning up dead or miss..."

"I don't get it either, but we have to find Link and Dink; then, we have to convince their parents that they can't move," Tim said. He pointed in the direction of the Cemetery Hill Graveyard. "I've had this weird sensation all morning that some answers are over there." The duo dropped their bikes and walked around the side of the house.

The boys next found themselves standing over Head Chef Grumbel's tombstone looking at a phrase.

Tim read the sentiment out loud: *"Thin as a rail you may not have been; your look was that of whale, the result of a deadly sin. Just the same, you have my name."* Todd added: *"It's signed, Glinda Grumbel, a loving wife."*

"You have my name?" Tim said with his left hand caressing his chin, "hmm, it's strange that she would word it that way, huh?"

"Man, you're right. Maybe it's just a mistake."

Then, as if by divine intervention, thoughts of Miss Tester began to enter into Tim's brain and would not leave. "Todd, it's time to go to Miss Tester's; I know she's home. She can help us discover where Dink and Link are. I know it."

* * *

The Tenders stopped their trusty *Travelers* in front of Miss Tester's yellow-colored brick, ranch-style home in Lakewood estates. Her house rested at 1492 Columbus Drive on the same side of Lake Maggiore as Lakehood High School. Columbus Drive wrapped around roads named after explorers and conquerors like De Soto, Cortez, and Coronado. Her walkway ran from the street, straight—not curvy and uphill like Granny Hart's—to the doorway. There was a screen door in front of another door made of fine cherry wood. Tim knocked, and the boys were in luck: Miss Tester answered and invited them in.

She had only been back a short time and knew nothing of the terrible tragedies that had taken place in St. Petersburg, the place of her employment not her birth. She hadn't been born in any part of Florida, but in the next state due north, Georgia—Helen to be exact, where she had recently been visiting her sick father. Her father was a veteran of the Korean War, where he had contracted *scrub typhus*. He was a gunnery sergeant in the Marines and had won the Congressional Medal of Honor. Thankfully, he would recover from his disease.

"Tim and Todd Tender, what a nice surprise! How are you boys?" the fifth-grade teacher said. She was twenty- nine years old and reminded the townsfolk of Vivien Leigh, who had won "best actress" for her role of Scarlett O'Hara in the movie *Gone With the Wind* in 1939. Mrs. Long, the sixth-grade teacher—the T&P gang's present grade—as a comparison, favored Margaret Hamilton. Margaret played the dual roles of the Wicked Witch of the West and Miss Gulch in *The Wizard of Oz,* also in 1939.

"Mi...Miss Test...Tester," Tim stammered. "We...we're glad yo...you're ho...home, huh?" He braced himself on the house.

"What's wrong? Slow down." Miss Tester patted Tim on the shoulder.

The gentle touch made things worse. "Li...nk and Di...nk are mis...sing; Car...Carl Steinberg and Gran...ny Hart are...are de...ad," Tim said as he smacked his face to try and fix his mouth.

"And so is Eddie Liebowitz, a kid from Palmetto," Todd added, then whispered to his brother. "Can the stutter, you sound like a drunk cockatoo."

"What the devil are you talking about? Who's dead and who's missing? Are you sure you've got the correct town? What's been happening in Saint Pete since I left? I can't believe what you're telling me."

"It's all true," Tim said, finally settling into a legible speech pattern, "we have a difficult time believing it, too, but our peaceful community has turned into a war zone. And nobody seems to have any clues. But, we have a theory, huh?"

"Obviously Daniels and Walker have no leads. Am I right?" the teacher said.

"Man, they think they do," Todd answered, "the law has Mrs. Grumbel tabbed as the killer. Can you believe that?"

"No." Miss Tester motioned toward her couch. "Sit down and tell me what you boys know."

"Well, we found, or I should say Todd found Eddie Liebowitz, a cub scout from Palmetto; he was drow...dead and still wearing his blue uniform."

"How gruesome! Where did you find the body?"

"Man, he was in the bathtub at the Barren mansion," Todd said. He instantly put his hand over his lips, knowing that she wouldn't approve.

"The Barren mansion! What were you doing there? That house has been abandoned for years," Miss Tester said with a voice laced with reprimand.

The Tender twins admitted that they were checking out the Barrens' residence to use as a clubhouse. They didn't mention that Link or Dink had also been on the premises. They did tell the school instructor that the Liebowitz kid—just like the Barren youngsters—had had his right thumb and forefinger sliced-off, and his tongue was half gone, and that none of the body parts were ever located. This information combined with the circumstances surrounding Cookie's death, the Tenders told Tester, led Sheriff Daniels and Deputy Walker to arrest Mrs. Grumbel. They continued to tell her that Chef Grumbel's ghost—the T&P membership's choice for the killer—broke the little woman out of jail.

"Well, first of all, I do not accept the notion of ghosts existing in the real world." The elementary educator pointed toward her front picture window as if the *real world* was beyond the glass. "I am a purveyor of knowledge and believe there is a scientific explanation for everything."

The Tenders felt that she was wrong in her belief; it had been proven to them first hand. But, they did not dispute her opinion— they needed her help.

After receiving the facts about how Kim's cherished Carl was extinguished, Miss Tester arrived at some solutions of her own. "As I already know, the Barrens were each injected in the heart with hydrogen peroxide, which actually caused their deaths, not the dismemberments. The Liebowitz boy, as you told me, was drowned, and Carl's demise may have been, more than likely was, created by the carbon dioxide gas in his lungs. Does that sound correct to you two?"

"You get an A," Todd said.

Tim jumped up from the couch. "An A-plus-plus!"

"What about Granny Hart? You never told me how she died?"

Annie Tester walked into the kitchen and stopped in front of the fridge. "You boys want a Coke?"

"No thanks." Tim and Todd spoke together. "We just split a Pepsi."

"Shot in the back of the neck with a small-caliber bullet," Tim began explaining, "the medical examiner guessed that it came from a non-American-made gun."

"But, what was even more freaky was the black paint on the wall over the fireplace with the number '10' on one side and '11' on the other," Todd added.

"What?" Annie Tester ran back into the living room— her eyes brightening. "That's it."

"What's it?" the boys queried.

"They're all similar methods that the Nazis used to murder Jews and Poles, as well as others, in those awful concentration camps during World War II. It clicked when you mentioned the black paint and the numbers—that's describing the 'black wall of death' at Auschwitz-Birkenau, where horrible wickedness took place."

"**OH! NO!**" Tim screamed. "Of course, Mrs. Barren's uncle from Warsaw, Liebowitz, Steinberg, it all fits; someone is trying to get rid of the Jewish and Polish people in St. Petersburg."

"But what about Granny? She wasn't a Jew or a Pole, was she?" Todd questioned.

"No, she wasn't, but a fanatic of this magnitude would destroy anyone or anything that got in *its* way. There are no total allegiances in these situations, although they'd try to tell you otherwise."

"Well, who in this town would follow such Nazi garbage?" Todd asked as he pinched his nose.

"*Mein Kampf! Mein Kampf!* that book, that's it, that awful book sits in Principal Coffery's file cabinet like it was a trophy,"

Tim said. "I saw it once when I got swats for something I didn't do." Neither Todd or Miss Tester paid any attention to Tim's last statement.

"I always felt there was something fishy about Deacon Coffery, the way he blew into town and started to take over. I was always unsuccessful in trying to get the school board to check out his background. I never liked him, but I didn't think him capable of something like this."

"Hey, Judy Goldberg, Coffery was there when she got sick, too," Todd said, "he probably tried to poison her food that day."

Just then, Annie Tester left the room and returned a moment later with a pearl-handled six gun strapped to each one of her legs. She had decided to assist the Tenders. And there wasn't any indication that she thought it necessary to contact the *Bourbon Kings*, Daniels and Walker. She felt that they would just get in the way and botch up the rescue effort.

"Can you handle those pistols?" Tim asked pointing to the guns.

"Are you a cowgirl as well as a teacher?" Todd said.

"Yup! my parents named me Annie and wanted me to learn how to protect myself. Before I graduated with a degree in Education from the University of Georgia as a *bulldog*, I attended the Annie Oakley Fast-Draw-and-Straight-Shootin' Institute in Ohio. I can shoot from a horse or a bicycle and hit any object just as easy with a mirror as without.

I always wanted to join the Ringling Brothers, Barnum, & Bailey Circus and become a star attraction like Annie Oakley had been in Buffalo Bill's Wild West Show. I can definitely handle these six-shooters." She grabbed each pearl handle but didn't draw the pistols—yet. "We need some concrete evidence that Link and Dink are trapped at Coffery's place before we go chargin' in."

Tim was really encouraged by Miss Tester's attitude, and he could see progress in the pursuit of the two absent club members.

The band of three piled into Annie Tester's Ford—bought from Dad Tender and painted the same red, white, and blue colors as the T&P gang's Schwinn *Traveler* bikes. They left Columbus Drive and steamed toward Serpentine Circle and a date with a principal gone mad—and his brainwashed secretary.

Chapter 26

"*Frau* Coffery, it is time to wake the young Jews and show them the 'trophy room,'" *Herr* Coffery beckoned, "cuff and blindfold them."

Eve completed the command; then, pushed the Playlen twins with a black lacquered rod down the "hall of fame" anteroom toward the end and turned them to the left at Hitler's black-red-and-white portrait. She raised her right hand in the direction of the Leader's face. Link and Dink were facing a set of French-style double doors that were locked. They couldn't see a thing. Eve removed—ungently—the blindfold from each twin's scared face.

The doors flung open and there stood the Principal... Deacon Coffery...PegLeg...the *Kommandant*...he had many aliases. And apparently no one knew the real designation that was listed on his birth certificate. He was flaunting his Nazi best: visor cap with the skull 'n' crossbones overtop the swastika; German medals above the left pocket; gold ribbon from right shoulder to iron-crossed right breast; the ivory-gripped, acorn-studded hunting knife; and a luger, which was strapped to his right leg opposite the blade.

"Welcome to the 'trophy room,'" the *Kommandant* said, "the room of which I am most proud." He was beaming.

"*Ja*, all the items that you will observe in this special place were gathered by friends of the cause," *Frau* Eve said, holding her arms out as if she was going to hug imaginary people.

After the hand checks were removed, each boy was deposited in a desk, the same type that was used at Lakeside Elementary. Link was sitting at a desk with his name, LINK PLAYLEN, carved into it. The words DINK PLAYLEN were chiseled into the school seat that Dink was forced into.

"Where the...did you get these?" Dink said as he slouched down in the desk. His brother did the same. It was as if they were defying an order from one of their teachers.

The first thing that caught each Playlen twin's eyes was the nine-branched *Hanukkah menorah*. Inside the eight holders—four on each side of the *shammes*—was either a human thumb or a human forefinger. And in the middle, the *shammes* was stuffed with someone's entire forearm, wrist, and hand. The detached body parts were dark blue and severely bruised.

The boys were shoved—with *Frau* Coffery's prodding poker—closer to the awful sacrilege. As they were pulling their desks awkwardly along the floor, they noticed the number "756" on the forearm. The *shammes* was normally used to hold the candle that lit the candles in the remaining holders. The *menorah* was sitting squarely in the midsection of the mantel above the fireplace.

Over the shelf, a red-and-white prison uniform was enclosed inside an expensive-looking gold frame. The "756" figure again was evident—this time with a red triangle overshadowing the dig-its—on the left side of the striped coat and the right leg of the pants. The next thing that the twins were coerced into looking at was half of a tongue floating in some sort of liquid that made it appear almost alive. The bottle containing the taste bud organ was resting to the left of the Jewish candelabrum...on the right was a glass Mason jar consisting of two gold teeth.

The boys were then brusquely turned around so that they were facing the opposite side of the room. There were four flags on the wall. The twins recognized all the flags from studies in Miss Tester's class on World History.

The quartet of banners had been placed on the wall in the form of a square: Nazi swastika on the top left; black-red-and-yellow German flag on the top right; navy blue-and-white—Star of David—flag of Israel on the bottom left; and red-and-white emblem of Poland on the bottom right. The two lower ones were seared and frayed.

The kids also saw a dark red cape with hood hanging on a coat rack in the corner.

"Impressive, don't you agree, young Jews?" *Kommandant* Coffery said as he finished a 180-degree twirl.

It hit the Playlens directly in the face harder than when Rocco Francis Marchegiano—known to most as "Rocky" Marchiano—knocked out Jersey Joe Walcott in 1952 for the heavyweight championship of the boxing world. Had this person, the present principal of their beloved Lakeside school, been murdering humans for years? It was difficult to grasp, but Coffery's so-called "trophy room" held all the evidence needed to point to him as the killer.

Link leaned a little to the left and whispered into his brother's right ear, "How do you think he got her to help him?"

"Beats the cra...outa me. Nope, no more swearing!"

The Playlens had talked earlier about playing along with their captors—a plan devised to avoid further loss of the community's citizens: specifically, Link and Dink.

"Now you will learn about the process that I, *The Kommandant,* used to procure these marvelous items for my one-of-a-kind room." His arms were opened wide as if welcoming family members.

"A brilliant game plan, my *Kommandant*," *Frau* Coffery said with an adoring tone in her voice.

"To help mastermind my strategy, I needed to recruit a subordinate who would become loyal to the cause and assist me in gaining financial backing, which is desperately needed when improving the shape of the world. Eve," he pointed toward his secretary, "was a logical choice for a deputy... she had no *choice*. But now she has fully embraced the return of the master race to its proper place in the universe."

"**Heil Hitler!**" the *Frau* screamed, right hand and arm extended up in the familiar pose.

"She's wonderful, isn't she boys?"

"The *Untermenschen* will die; subhumans like you twin Jews will cease to exist on the face of the earth," *Frau* Eve said with a conviction that made Link and Dink realize that she had flown over the edge just like PegLeg.

"Before I start—Dink, I bring you deepest regards from Lorraine via the lovely city of Three Egg. My dear daughter says she misses you very much."

"No way!" Dink returned. He sat straight up in the desk. "Lorraine would never have told you about u..."

"You're right, I haven't spoken to her since she left here. Were you stupid enough to think I wouldn't find out about the two of you?"

"And Link," Eve interrupted, "Lorraine also wishes that she could come back and visit Denington's with you for another soda-fountain tryst."

"Yes," Deacon Coffery added, holding a pair of fingers up, "she enjoyed your two-straw rendezvous. In the same glass— how romantic."

"How did you know ab..."

"Oh, we know everything; it's our job to know," *Frau* Coffery said with confidence.

"**Link! what are they talking about?**" Dink cried, staring darts as his twin. "**You and Lorraine were together at Denington's?**"

"Dink, Dink, settle down; it was nothing. I didn't want you to get upset, so I didn't tell you. Besides, she was leaving town and that was the end of it. Forget her, she's not worth it, she's a floozie. Did you know that Tim towed her home on his bike one day?" Link's hands grabbed imaginary handlebars.

"**What, Tim, too?** What kind of friend and brother do I have? And she's not a floo..."

"**Alright!**" Coffery pounded his fist down on Dink's desk. The boys jumped, startled. "That's enough. I need to begin. Your friend, Mrs. Barren's uncle, was our first conquest...yes, that's right, the uncle from Warsaw. We never had him in the camp in Poland where I worked during the war—one of the few to escape proper justice. That situation was rectified."

"That's right, you little Jew creeps," the *Frau* stuck her face directly in front of Link's, "Deacon was deputy *Kommandant* at one of Hitler's finest concentration camps; though, he was the real leader. A sort of all-seasons' fun park."

Coffery started to pace. "*Der Fuehrer's* 'Final Solution' had to be continued, so we forced the uncle to watch the elimination of his family by injections; then, arranged their bodies in such a manner as to appear subhuman...which, partly thanks to him, they were. Messy business. A case of being in the wrong place at the wrong time. And the children were of no medical use."

"The right place at the right time, I'd say," Eve added, as she *heiled* to the Nazi flag, one of many that seemed to be in every room of the mansion.

The Playlen twins weren't saying a word but felt that St. Sid's would have two people here that could easily get their own special wing at the asylum—patients who could move directly to the head of the class. The twins' lives now probably depended on their judgmental silence.

"I had to use hydrogen peroxide for the injections into the hearts; I wanted to apply phenol, a quicker remedy. I used the white crystalline product in Poland for past triumphs but could not find any locally."

"And as you two know, the peroxide worked just fine," Eve chimed, "I wish I could have been in town to help on that case. As Deacon has told me, *Herr* Wolf assisted nicely."

"He was enthralled by the expelling of the young Barrens and demanded that juvenile Jews be made an example," the *Kommandant* said. "Judy Goldberg was my first attempt, a failed attempt—not enough dosage of C-B pellets. He was not happy. Judy so wanted to be the boss of the baton-twirling team; it's all that she could think of."

"Too...o...ba...a...ad," *Frau* Eve crooned as she caught a make-believe baton out of her brainwashed air.

"So, you made Judy sick, not Head Chef Grumbel; aren't you clever," Link said.

"Tim was right about the Chef not being responsible for that," Dink added.

"Fooled you, huh?" Coffery said.

"Not very hard to do with dumb Jews," Eve Coffery interjected. "And, as luck would have it, little Eddie Liebowitz showed up later with his mother on the Lakeside doorstep. She didn't want him to go to the school in Palmetto. We got his address right off the application. It was as easy as pie to *snatch* him," she performed the movement like Eddie was in the room, "right out of the Liebowitz's front yard...nobody the wiser. Just drove the car up, opened the passenger door, flashed some sourball candy, and seized the little prince." She pulled the identical hard sweets out of her pocket that she kept there for nice surprises and offered some to the Playlen boys. They refused. "For hours his parents didn't even know he was gone. He was so cute in his cub scout uniform."

"Yes, things aren't always greener on the other side, sometimes they're red," Principal Coffery said. "Drowning was the method of choice for young Eddie. That wonderful wash tub in your present home-away-from-home...my *castle keep*...served our purpose well. And don't you think it was a stroke of genius to place the body in the Barrens' bathtub? He provided that idea. I had the kid's blue-and -yellow scarf as a prize but lost it. I can't imagine where? Oh, well, maybe it will turn up some day."

"He? Who's the 'he' you keep referring to?" Link asked.

"Doesn't matter, it's not important; but, I needed his extra strength to subdue the next victim. Kim Tender's boyfriend—the late, great 'Cookie' Steinberg."

"Show them the murder weapon, *Herr Kommandant*," Eve said with anticipation, pointing toward the door.

In the next instant, the twins were pulled out of the school chairs; pushed out the double doors; shoved through the Nazi-monster's hallway down a short flight of stainless steel stairs; and flung into an iron door. There was a round crank on the metal portal, and Coffery turned it counterclockwise. Together, he and

124

Eve strained to pull back the heavy door. When it eventually opened, a garage appeared behind it. A black VW Beetle and another car, which was covered up with a ragged piece of canvas, became evident.

"This is a 1938 Volkswagen that came from a factory, where *Der Fuehrer* himself spoke at the opening of the plant. Impressive, no?" Coffery walked the twins around to the front of the round, buggy-looking auto. The boys each noticed the word "Porsche" on the front license plate. "You should be proud...many of your ancestors, along with Russians and Poles, helped build this affordable car for the German people. And, an idea—the assembly line—that our Leader was astute enough to take from the USA's Henry Ford—worked well with our laborers."

"You mean slave laborers," Link whispered to his identical sibling.

"What? I didn't understand you."

"Nothing."

"Show them the killing weapon," Eve said impatiently.

Deacon Coffery pulled back the cloak from the other car. A hot rod with reddish-orange flames stretching the whole length of the vehicle was revealed. The windows were dark and the interior was not visible.

Both Dink and Link immediately realized that this was the car that Mrs. Grumbel had claimed ran her and Mr. Grumbel off Twenty-fifth Street...causing his death and her disfigurements.

"What's this hot rod have to do with Cookie's death?" Dink said as he aimed a finger at it.

"All we had to do is leave the car in an abandoned parking lot....He was drawn to it like it was a magnet and he had a metal plate lodged in his head," the *Frau* beamed.

Link said, "But, Cookie wasn't run down; he was found in the lake drow..."

"Ah, that's just the place where you," Coffery waving a fist at Dink, "discovered the body. Intruding where you didn't belong."

"Thanks to you, you little Jew creep," Mrs. Coffery interjected, "we lost a couple of good items for the 'trophy room,' but I was able to regain some suitable replacements."

"From who?" the boys said in unison.

"Later."

"I didn't have time to do the decapitation, either. He wanted the head," the *Kommandant* moved a finger across his neck, "for something special. Never told me for what."

Eve explained to the Playlens that Carl had been knocked unconscious and placed in the hot rod; then, a large rag was stuffed into the exhaust pipe, and the engine was cranked up. "The garage was sealed so tight that even the great Houdini couldn't have escaped."

It was also spelled out that the removal of the right thumbs and forefingers from the corpses was to point suspicion in the direction of Head Custodian Grumbel. And, as Eve so graciously indicated, the plan worked—a*ka*, Sheriff Daniels and Deputy Walker.

Playing along with the lunacy that he was hearing, Link said, "Okay, removing the fingers and thumbs from three cadavers only adds up to six. Where did the other two in the sacred *menorah* come from?" Link was disgusted with what the Nazi sweethearts were using the holy candelabrum for; he knew that his twin brother felt the same way.

"I'll let *Frau* Coffery explain that; after all, she's responsible for acquiring the final fingers. She performed her initial test beautifully. Eve," he gently caressed her arm, "the floor is yours."

"*Merci, Her...*"

"**No**! Eve, it's *danke schon*."

"Sorry, *danke schon, Herr Kommandant*."

"Don't let it happen again. Continue."

"Your crackpot friend, Granny Hart, provided the last candle fillers; she was butting in where she didn't belong. A bullet to the back of the neck from Deacon's nine-millimeter luger did the trick—or, should I say treat."

"Old lady Hart's clairvoyance apparently wasn't working too well that night; she never saw it coming," *Herr* Coffery added. "The old bag called here and threatened me...bad move on her part."

"All she was interested in was getting rid of those chocolate-covered bugs; *Herr* Wolf took care of those," Eve said.

"What did she try to threaten you with?" Dink asked as he leaned on the hot rod. His brother had a leg up on the chrome bumper. They were still playing along.

"Said she got a message fro..."

"From the 'other side,'" Deacon Coffery said, a smirk widening on his face.

"That's right, whatever that is...said she knew all that we were doing and was going to take the proper measures to stop it. Well, I showed her some of my lethal action," she made a trigger-pulling motion. "As demented as she was, she's better off now."

The Playlen twins were again handcuffed and blindfolded and taken back to their casket holding-cells.

Link and Dink later told Tim that when they were finally back in their coffins, they were terrified. They were completely convinced that PegLeg and Eve were definitely crazy. The Nazi and the Nazi *wannabe* talked about the awful crimes like it was a duty enjoyed and not enforced by some overseer. There never was any remorse visible.

Because of the holes in their coffins, the boys could talk to each other. The frightened duo decided to converse about their favorite holidays and some of the great stories that existed about them. Hopefully, for at least a little while, they could forget about the dangerous situation that they were entangled in, and take their minds, if not their bodies, away from this place of doom.

Tim told me (the Red Sox guy, remember?) that Link and Dink's parents, Mom being of Jewish faith and Dad a Catholic, decided to raise their children exposing them to both religions. And, although weekends at two services were busy for the kids, the situation, occurrences of the *Porky Spence* type being minimal, was working out fine. Especially considering, at the time, only one of ten marriages in America had interfaith as a part of its makeup.

Chapter 27

Christmas was the first holiday discussed. December Twenty-fifth had always been a wonderful day for Link and Dink Playlen. The gift tradition in their family was to open one present on the Eve of Christmas and the rest on the "Day." As a comparison, at Tim and Todd's home, no presents were opened the night before. The giving-and-receiving ritual was a high priority in each of the household's holiday season. All four members of the T&P club never could contain their excitement in anticipation of the Santa Claus arrival—even though they were smart enough to know that their parents were just playing the part of Saint Nicholas— kind of down-to-earth elves. Just the same, they always left milk and cookies for *the Big Christmas Kahuna* and his helpers, and biscuits for Frisky the reindeer... that is, before he became lost.

Although, Tim frequently tells a mysterious tale about one Christmas Eve when a very extraordinary and wonderful thing took place:

The entire Tender clan was going to their church's midnight services. Before departing, Todd and Tim followed custom: Borden's, homemade peanut butter cookies, and dog treats were left on a small wooden table next to the evergreen.

When the family returned from Fifth Avenue Baptist, there were presents strategically placed on the previously bare floor under the bubble-lighted tree. The Yuletide lumber had been dark when they departed. The refreshments as well as the canine biscuits were gone. Frisky was fast asleep in his doggie bed with a smile showing wide under his whiskers. And, finally, many white strands of human hair were on display throughout the living room. Not one Tender had such a color on their domes.

No explanation for these strange string of events was ever exposed.

Because Erik Playlen was not of Jewish ancestry, as Golda was, the Playlens celebrated two holidays in December/Kislev: Christmas and Hanukkah.

The Playlens annually invited the Tenders to share in the celebration of the Eight-Day Festival of Lights, and the invitation was always accepted gratefully.

"Remember the year we all got our Schwinn's?" Dink asked.

"Yea, you were like a proud peacock riding over to Tim and Todd's to show off your new blue bike," Link said with a wide grin growing on his face that his twin couldn't see.

"And we get there only to find out they have the same bikes, only whi..."

"Imagine that."

"Biking instead of walking's great."

"We sure can cover a bunch more ground," Link said, trying to sound untroubled.

"At least our bikes are safe and sound," Dink added. He moved inside his coffin and nails scratched his body. "Ow! Watch those nails, Link. I guess we just have to stay still."

"Ri...ri...right," Link returned, shivering as he talked, "I wi...wish Coffery would give us back our shirts." He tried to ignore the coldness in the room. "I hope my bike's okay; it's down the street in some bushes. Remember the first place we all went when we got our Schw..."

"Yea, man, 'The Day After Christmas Discount Sale' at Webb's. Great bargains on gifts for the following December Twenty-fifth."

"You know, Dink, when we get out of here...and we will, trust me...I think we ought to give all those presents to the charity at the Tenders' church for underprivileged families."

"Man, that's a great idea."

"Do you think the Nazis celebrated Christmas?"

"Link, do you remember when we each got our first *dreidl* toy for *Hanukkah* and Tim and Todd couldn't figure out how to use it or what the phrase *Nes Gadol Po* meant?"

"Yea, and when they finally realized it was a spinning toy, we told them that the slogan from Israel stood for 'A Great Miracle Happened Here.'"

"What did Tim say? 'Oh, how appro...'"

"'Oh, how appropriate' is what he said. That was a scream," Link said, almost laughing out loud.

"They couldn't believe the operation was so simple; instead, they thought it would almost take a miracle to figure it out," Dink said.

"I love the *dreidl*."

"Me too."

"The Tenders were so excited when Mom and Pop let them each light a candle on the *menorah* on successive days."

"You could tell that they really respected the process of lighting the candles and what it all represented."

"And it was great the way they were fascinated by the story behind the *Hanukkah Menorah* about the two great miracles," Link said.

"Right, it's a wonderful tale of courage and determination about the Maccabees and Mattathias, their father. Did you know that Mom told me that after the Syrian ruler Antiochus IV corrupted and stripped the Temple of Jerusalem, Mattathias and his five sons, Judah, Johanan, Simon, Jonathan, and Eliezer, normally peace-loving farmers, became great warriors? And even though the Syrian army was much larger, better-trained, and better-armed, their Jewish counterparts fought as guerillas in the mountains. And with Judah as the new leader after the father died in 166 B.C.E, seized back control of the Temple in 165 B.C.E," Dink said with respect in his voice.

"Mom told me the same story and what's sad is that the father, Mattathias, wasn't able to share in the celebration of the

Jews' independence from the Syrians because of dying the year before."

"But, Judah, man, Judah took over the reins and did those stupid Syrians i..."

"Yea, chased them back where they belonged."

"To have been there when they rededicated the Temple of God and the Eight-Day Festival continued on. That would've been great."

Link responded to Dink when he reminisced about Tim's reaction to the second miracle. "Do you recall what Tim said about when the Jews cleaned the temple to purify it and found only enough holy oil for one day's burning?"

"'Eight days! No way it could have burned for eight days' is what he said, and he, as well as Todd, agreed that those truly were two of the grand miracles."

"That's what angers me about the *Menorah* that sits in Coffery's so-called 'trophy room,'" Link said, disgusted.

"I can't believe he would desecrate the meaning of the Jewish candelabrum the way he di..."

"True enough; but, what he and Eve put into the holders and the death left as a result of their insanity is much worse than mistreating the sanctity of the *Menorah*."

"You're absolutely right, but I don't want to think about that now or whether we're going to become part of the lineup of doom that these two freaks and the 'he' Coffery keeps talking about have been bringing down on the Jews and Poles of this town."

"Yea, just who could this 'he' be, anyway?" Link asked.

"I don't know. Tell me about the egg hunt you all had at Lakeside that Easter when I was in Mound Park," Dink said with anxiety, trying to forget their predicament.

"That stomach virus was serious; we were lucky you made it through that okay. No thanks to that imbecile in the emergency room that said you only had the flu. Thank goodness for Doctor Kidd, who put you in the hospital immediately after his diagnosis."

"Yea, remember, it got much worse the next day; the Doc said any more delay and I could have died. Enough about that morbid stuff, tell me about the search for the Easter Eggs."

Before starting the story, Link told his brother that he thought that he heard some noise just outside their prison door.

Dink had already listened to the story many times but never got tired of it.

Link began:

Okay, most of the kids at Lakeside that year stayed up most of the eve of the Friday night that started the Easter weekend and colored eggs, thousands of them. The hen ovals, some dyed in colors not known to science, were brought to school and given to the teachers to hide for the Saturday hunt. Little sleep by the students was the order of the egg-enhancing evening—the excitement was running too high.

The day of the big search finally arrived and kids showed up in droves promptly at 9:16 in the morning. Not one was late. Supposedly, the playing field had not been touched or viewed since the teachers had sprinkled the area with the multi-colored shells of kiddies' delight.

Everyone started out in the school cafeteria. A whistle worn around the neck of Mrs. Strepp, the fourth-grade teacher, was blown, and kids broke through the doors like a herd of American buffalo on stampede caused by death-defying hunters shooting at the once peacefully-grazing bison. The ready-set-go assignment was usually performed by the principal, but that year Coffery was a no-show. Said he had a sore throat.

The Lakesiders hunted and hunted and hunted but couldn't find a single egg. After thirty minutes of hard-boiled disappointment, the kids all filed back into the cafeteria and wanted some answers about the concealed Easter treasures.

Had the instructors hidden the valuables too well?
Were they playing games?

The adults and children, as one huge mass, trudged back down to the playground section of the schoolyard and began a second search. Knowing exactly where they had laid the eggs, the older humans felt that they could locate the gems without a hitch.

Wrong!

Not a reddish-orange, red, green, black, pink, violet, yellow, striped, gold, or even a plain white egg was found.

Very curious.

In the next moment, the Streppster, as some of the students were fond of calling her, cried to the top of her voice that there was a dead alligator—not Big Alvin—lying on the northwest bank of Lake Maggiore. The reptile was absolutely stiff.

The local veterinarian, a Seminole Indian living and working in St. Petersburg, was summoned; he carted the gator away in his pick-up truck that had the same slogan on both doors:

IF YOUR ANIMAL IS LOST, SICK, OR DEAD, DOCTOR BOWDEN WILL SEEK, TREAT, OR IMPLANT WITH A HEART.

The Saturday was ruined and all the people who showed for the Easter festivities went home depressed.

A strange thing happened the next day. Dr. Bowden informed the townspeople that when he opened up the alligator's stomach with his scalpel, at least one thousand eggs—maybe two thousand—all of which were still in their original shapes and colors, were resting comfortably in the reptile's abdomen.

The two questions that floated around town for years: With a fence surrounding the entire lake, how did the alligator get the gorgeous ovals, and how could the eggs not have been chewed?

"That was great," Dink said. "Weird about those eggs."

"You still enjoy that story even after the eighth telling?"

"It never gets old."

"Okay, now you tell me about the Passover incident," Link said with anticipation.

"You mean the year that Porky Spence came to the first day of the celebration with a ham?"

"Yea, cool, that one! Ow!" Link got too excited and was pricked by the confining nails.

"Careful. Dad said that the ham looked deliciously fresh and succulent, even with the cloves sticking out of it. He told everyone that the brown sugar, butter, and maple syrup topping was whispering his name over and over: 'Erik, Erik, have some, go ahead and dig in, you'll be sorry if you don't. Trust me, the saucy sauce that's presently calling you home, this lovely pinkish pork meat won't last forever.'"

"If he would've just ate the ham, tho..." Link said.

"Right, but during the *seder*, when he put the meat, along with giant globs of mustard and mayonnaise on the *matzo*, Mom went through the roof." Dink paused for a moment and chuckled to himself. "She yelled at him about how during their escape from Egypt led by Moses, the Israelites didn't prepare the unleavened bread to eat throughout the eight-day observance and then pass down the tradition through time so that he could slap meat from a filthy pig on the sacred bread and douse it with messy condiments."

"He never did anything like that again," Link said.

"Remember the secret he told us?" Dink asked.

"You mean the secret about the knife he used to spread the mayo and mustard? That he didn't boil it first."

"Yea, that's the on..."

Suddenly, the lids from both Link's and Dink's caskets flew open with an ungodly force.

Chapter 28

Some *thing* wearing a black-hooded cape seized Link and yanked him out of the coffin like it was ripping a page out of a book. A moving crimson cloak which also had a cowl, performing as quickly as a shell shot from a luger, grabbed Dink and threw him down on the slippery concrete floor. The Playlens were reintroduced to the handcuffs and blindfolds—now, it seemed, a part of their body makeup.

The next road trip they were sent on was down spiral stairs...many stairs...winding, winding, winding. The two caped individuals shoved the twins against walls, stone walls that were uneven with sharp chunks protruding from the surface. Semi-tough skin was scraped from the arms and chests of the boys. No remorse was shown by the human pushing-machines.

Farther and farther the foursome descended; the atmosphere became cold, as cold as the metal slabs where countless corpses spend dead days inside the frigid cabinets of any morgue. The two young boys—shirtless and shoeless— were freezing, actually shaking, teeth chattering and sounding like an out-of-control telegraph.

Their caped captors strolled as if it was a lovely spring afternoon.

The downward decline finally ended with Link and Dink being shoved into a huge metal door containing a round handle—much like the one that led to the garage—situated squarely in the middle.

The Playlens' eye masks were torn off. The black hood attached to the cape of its wearer was now resting comfortably on the individual's back.

The face was exposed.

Surprise!

It was Deacon Coffery.

The twins didn't need to speculate as to the identity of the crimson-covered guard: it was Eve.

The hand restraints were removed and the twins were forced to turn the metal handle clockwise. The rotation was difficult and when the process didn't continue as quickly as she liked, Mrs. Coffery stuck each kid in the back with her pointed rod. After she assisted the boys with incessant poking, the twins worked the crank free and the door opened. What appeared behind it looked like a rough version of a medical lab. There were two shiny steel tables with leather straps—two on either side of each table for a total of eight. The belts were stretching toward another concrete floor, this deck spattered with many spots colored red. A l s o , the room contained *Bunsen* burners firing away, some topped with glass bowls filled with bubbling liquid; *IV* poles with plastic bags attached; and scalpels, syringes, and rubber gloves everywhere.

Then, the boys were exposed to a scene that made them dry heave uncontrollably for what seemed like forever:

There was a separate table, a table constructed of polished marble with several sinks attached that held metal taps. *Not* the table but what was on it caused the twins' spontaneous illness: a cadaver split wide open from the bottom of its neck to the tip of its umbilicus. Entrails, intestines…organs and more organs were draped over the outside of the cavity as if a hand grenade had gone off inside and blown the innards outward.

The thing that made it worse was that the face—the only identifiable part—belonged to Granny Hart.

"Where," Link said to his captors, pointing toward the destroyed corpse, "did you get Mrs. Hart's body?"

"**And what have you done to her?**" Dink screamed with a look of terror on his face.

"A little financial persuasion thrown in the direction of the funeral director, who seems to always be in need of money, provided what I needed for my research," the self- proclaimed Nazi doctor answered smugly.

Before they had time to grieve for the local medium— whom the twins hoped was now secure with Harvey Hart—Link and Dink were strapped, each one to a table, tighter than a lady's corset drawn to its stomach-stuffing limit.

"To begin," Deacon Coffery said, now sans the black cape and dressed in a white medical coat and wearing white rubber gloves, "a little experiment in the transfer of pain from one identical twin to the other." Eve, still wearing her red robe, assisted the doctor?

Dink Playlen, because of his nasty mouth, was used as the *control* twin.

A request by Eve.

Granted! by her husband and superior.The fingernail from Dink's right forefinger was removed slowly by one of the razor-sharp scalpels taken from the instrument tray. Nurse Eve had previously stuffed a handkerchief overloaded with swastikas into Dink's mouth. Link's blindfold was placed back over his eyes, and earplugs—a new toy—were stuck deep into his ears. Blood spurted from Dink's finger and he screamed a bloody scream that his twin didn't seem to sense in any manner. Link, not able to hear or see what was going on, didn't utter a sound. The insanity continued when another cuticle was cut and a second nail was taken away from the "bird" finger.

Even though he could not discern anything, Link spoke: "What are you doing to my brother?" It was the wrong thing to say....He should have yelled to the top of his voice, as if in gruesome pain like his twin sibling, a brother that he loved very much. Maybe that would have stopped the pair of Nazi-loving freaks; but, he hadn't felt any anguish. A third and fourth nail and, finally, the thumbnail were all separated from Dink's non-throwing hand.

Nobody in the makeshift medical lab was even aware that Dink had passed out after the second nail was displaced. What Deacon and Eve Coffery had realized, though, was that Link Playlen never once delivered a peep of pain.

"Dr. Coffery," the *frau* suggested to her honeymoon partner, "maybe we've chosen the wrong twin to be the *control* subject."

"Possibly," Coffery turned toward his little woman, "you are correct."

The *swastika* rag was immediately discharged from Dink's mouth and crammed into Link's; Link's blindfold and earplugs—just as quickly—became Dink's property. The fake MD and his dangerous second-in-command were in such a frenzied state that they still hadn't recognized that Dink was unconscious.

Coffery used his German hunting knife, ground to such a fine edge that it was even sharper than the scalpels. He didn't waste time with Link's fingernails; instead, the maniac sliced off the whole tip of the pinky on Link's left hand, hoping that the agony would transfer to Dink. The red stuff was flowing freely, young Link cried in torment, and he, too, lost consciousness. Finally, the two adult incompetents figured that the experiment was a failure and terminated the operation.

Nurse Coffery applied a coagulant to Link's littlest digit then sewed up the hole. Dink's hand had not bled enough to require clotting. Anesthetics had never been administered—a wonderful testament to the duo of self-declared Nazi healers.

"These twins are strong," Coffery said as he flexed his biceps, "there is no need to build their strength. It's time for the 'vivo stage.' In their present condition the figures we need will come much easier."

During the "vivo stage," Eve performed the tasks of measuring Dink's and Link's noses, eyes, ears, and other outward features of their bodies. She also gauged, meticulously, the distance between each body part: nose to ear, ear to ear, eye to eye, eye to nose—dimensions were taken in every conceivable direction that ended with the tape measure extended from the middle of each kid's forehead around the skull and back to the identical spot where the procedure started.

Both Eve and Deacon were astonished that in every case, with the exception of the nose calculations, the results were exactly the same. Dink had had his sniffer broken and pushed to one side in 1953 trying to do a handstand on his Schwinn while the bike was moving. Ironically, at the time, he was showing off for Principal Coffery's daughter, Lorraine.

"*Frau* Coffery, apply the smelling salts!" the doctor raved, "it will bring the young Jews around and we can then test them for their pain thresholds."

"Do you mean electric shock treatments?" Eve begged gleefully as she picked up the restorative capsules.

"*Ja!*"

"*Heil*, **Hitler!**"

Chapter 29

Link's dented canteen, spied and recovered by Tim from under one of Coffery's leafy oleander bushes, was enough proof to convince Annie Tester. Sporting a Samuel Colt revolver tied to each leg, she and the twins decided to enter the mausoleum in search of the two lost students. The trio had to find the easiest entrance into the evil house and hope that they wouldn't be discovered.

* * *

When Dink and Link finally came around long after the excruciating experiments were over, each one experienced a fresh ache—coming from his left forearm.

"Dink, does your left arm hurt?"

"Yea, very much, Link."

The casket tops were gently, not forcefully, pulled open.

"How are you kids feeling? We thought you would never wake up, missing the fun that's in store for the two of you," the doctor said, almost sounding sympathetic. Coffery was still donning his surgical whites.

In the next moment, *Frau* Eve entered the room wearing a blue skirt, white blouse with a brown vest over the shirt, and heavy boots and socks. "Can we start our next round of study now, Deacon? I'm anxious to continue."

"Yes, I am also eager. But, before we start with the shock treatments, I want to retrieve some bl...." Before he could finish his sentence, the doctor was interrupted by a twin.

"What's the 'ZW-1' that's on my arm?" Link said staring at his forearm in disbelief.

"Yea, mine says 'ZW-2' and it hurts almost as bad as my hand," Dink responded with an identical puzzled expression.

"Oh, that stands for *Zwillinge*, the German word for 'twin'; I tattooed those markings there just in case you got lost, you could be identified," Dr. Coffery stated. "Nurse Coffery, it's time to draw the blood."

"*Ja!* I have the ten cc. syringe ready." She stuck a needle into Dink, then Link.

After the amateurish transfusion, not another drop of blood would drain from either Playlen's right arm. Luckily, the fanatic vampira in the female Nazi youth costume couldn't find a vein in Link's or Dink's left arm. Once again the two boys became one with their dreams.

* * *

Miraculously, the garage door of the Coffery crypt was open, and the three hopeful rescuers entered the auto shelter without a hitch.

Something strange about the back driveway area had been unmistakable: the climate was crisp, almost cold, except in the small section just outside where the vehicles were stored—there, it was warm.

Once inside, the trio moved beyond a black Beetle and another car that was covered with a canvas. Carefully, they climbed the stairs that led to a metal door that had a round crank. The garage was dark and damp. At this point, Miss Tester attempted to turn the handle.

"I can't manage it; you boys give it a go."

Tim tried.

Todd tried.

Still no luck.

"We can't open it, either."

It was as if Samson himself, long, wavy locks intact, had such a vice grip on the crank that not even the mighty Hercules could have budged it.

Suddenly, the air turned temperate again and the round metal grip spun around as smoothly as one of the Playlen *dreidls.* The door flew open. Annie, Todd, and Tim followed the moving mist through to the other side, where they encountered another short flight of stairs, ones made of stainless steel.

The area that they came across at the top of the steps was *Kommandant* Coffery's "Hall of Fame" with paintings of the Nazi artisans of genocide.

The warm, sweet breeze immediately did a pivot to bitter cold, a coldness that instantly covered the entire hallway.

Because of Miss Tester's World History lessons, the three uninvited guests recognized the subjects of each picture, headed-up by *Der Fuehrer.* The problem presented was that not one of the liberators was anticipating such an awful array of Nazi monsters; they all stopped dead-in-their-tracks and stared in horror.

"The truth is becoming painfully evident," Tim said reluctantly, "Principal Deacon Coffery doubles as Nazi Deacon Coffery."

"Or more likely," Todd offered, "Deacon Coffery SS, became the leader of Lakeside."

Miss Tester took her eyes away from the Nazi fiends and turned toward her students. "And declared himself an American war hero."

The trio of emancipators came out of their stupor and Annie Tester continued, "You know, I always wondered about that terrible German propaganda book that Coffery keeps in his files; this evil display explains it."

"We have to put a stop to this plague," Tim said, boldness evident on his face.

The mild, clean air, once again, appeared and mobilized in a direction beyond the Adolf Hitler fiasco and toward another staircase, these steps traveling downward in a twisting manner. The triad followed the breeze without hesitation. They didn't know why but felt that it was taking them where they needed to go.

Down, down, down they went. Their descending dance ended abruptly at yet another metal door with a round crank. Because of the odd mix of warm and cold air, broad beads of sweat had developed on each forehead of the threesome. They continued on....

* * *

After about fifty percent of an hour passed from the twins' unwilling *KO*, the smelling salts were again administered.

Doctor Coffery had mutated back into *Kommandant* Coffery, decked-out in his dress uniform with weapons attached.

He began to translate passages from his favorite brainwashing book, *Mein Kampf*: "'If...the Jew conquers the nations of this world, his crown will become the funeral wreath of humanity, and once again this planet, empty of mankind, will move through the ether as it did thousands of years ago.' Is this not wisdom beyond reproach?"

"Don't forget what you taught me that *Herr* Himmler said, *Kommandant*," *Frau* Coffery added as she moved closer to the captives, "he stated, 'The struggle becomes fighting between the humans and subhumans.' And, as we all know, the 'humans' are the Germans and their backers and the 'subhumans' reflect the Jews, like you two cretins."

Before Coffery continued his reading, he told the twins that he and Eve had overheard some of their holiday conversation—and, that it was the principal and his secretary who had collected all the Easter eggs, greased them, and threw them in Lake Maggiore. They had been observing from an undetectable location where the teachers had hidden all the pretty chicken pearls.

The *Kommandant* started his sermonizing once more, and he and his wife worked themselves into such a delirium that neither one noticed that the round handle on the metal door was slowly twisting loose.

Coffery proceeded, now shouting, "**Lest we not forget what Goebbels so eloquently explained:** 'Our task here is surgical...drastic incisions, or some day Europe will perish of the Jewish disease.' Isn't the medical imagery marvelous?"

In the next minute, the door cleared and the three *deliverers-from-evil* appeared along with a wind that moved MD material from tables, trays, and tubes onto the crimson- blotted floor below.

"**Tim, Todd, and Mi..Mi..Miss Tester?**" the Playlen twins yelled in unison.

"**Wh...?**" Eve screamed as she retreated.

"**How did you three get in here?**" Coffery shouted, moving toward the trio. "**That door was twisted tight.**"

"Man, with a little help from a friend...I think?" Todd said.

"What have you done to Link and Dink, huh?" Tim asked, starting to get angry.

Annie Tester noticed the injuries that the Playlen twins had on a good portion of their mouths, arms, and hands. "**What in Heaven's name have you two morons been doing to these innocent children?**" The teacher put her hands closer to her pistols.

"You people don't belong here. My husband is carrying on very important research," Eve Coffery said with remarkable calm, "he can't afford any interruptions."

"Your husband? When did you two get married?" Tim said with each of his forefingers pointing at a different Coffery.

"Mr. and Mrs. Nazi Freak; man, sounds about right to me," Todd added as he smirked.

Out of heavy air, the book of Nazi testaments was knocked out of Coffery's hand and landed on the floor—the "knocker" was a mystery.

Annie Tester then proposed an ultimatum to *Kommandant* and *Frau* Coffery to release the battered Playlen boys or suffer the consequences from the quick draw of her pearl-handled *Colt's*. She also mentioned that she had finished third in her class at the Annie Oakley Institute.

Unfortunately, this fact didn't impress the *kommandant*—he raised the flap of his SS coat, unsnapped the part of his holster that covered the gun handle, and exposed his nine millimeter luger. "I also completed a quick draw course, at the University of Berlin; but, unlike you, Miss Tester, I ended second amongst the class competitors."

It was a showdown for the ages; but, unlike the legendary Wyatt Earp facing off with one of the Clanton boys at the O. K. Corral in Tombstone, Arizona, this one pitted a patriotic American against a Nazi, deranged beyond repair.

Kommandant Coffery—claiming head-of-the-household— explained the rules of the duel and told his wife, a union that the T&P members still couldn't comprehend, to count to three. The gunfighters would draw at the end of the last number.

Only, while he was clarifying the fight code, Coffery threw Eve a wink that only she could see. She knew exactly what he meant.

Not using good common sense, Annie took him at his word to draw after *three*. Instead, Coffery pulled his trigger after the second call from the lovable Eve, and a German bullet came speeding out of the barrel.

Suddenly, the warm and pure wind—that was earlier helping command the rescue effort—appeared before Annie Tester in the form of Head Chef Grumbel. The chef was holding the book, *Mein Kampf,* in front of his see-through body. The missile that was shot from the Nazi pistol entered the book's front flap, that covered page after page of evil tenets, and was stopped dead.

Immediately, Deacon Coffery revolved the weapon to shoot again; but, this time, Tim threw Eddie Liebowitz's blue-and-yellow cub scout scarf into the *kommandant's* area. The bandanna hit Coffery's hand and deflected the bullet directly into his newly-wed, right between her eyes. She dropped to the floor.

Coffery then circled his luger, many of which were made from the slave labor of countless Jewish and Polish prisoners, on himself and squeezed the trigger. The pistol blew up and severed the thumb and forefinger of his right hand. Without hesitation, he unsheathed his knife with his left five fingers and cut a hole in the leg of the SS pants that camouflaged his wooden limb. He flipped open the lid of a small compartment that had been carved in the honey maple, grabbed a pill, and popped it into his mouth. Within minutes, Deacon Coffery was on the red-spotted concrete floor twisting, turning, and trembling. After countless gyrations, his body finally quit.

What happened next completely terrified the remaining inhabitants that occupied *Kommandant* Coffery's torture chamber: a long, heavy, slimy-looking creature crawled out of the *kommandant's* body wearing PegLeg's *SS* uniform. It slinked toward the drain in the southeast corner of the room and just before it entered, the *thing* turned its head. It had a plain mug: a wide nose with a small, square, dark moustache running only the width of the bottom part of its snout; short hair parted on the right, pushed over and matted down to the left; and the most mesmerizing eyes, black eyes that could hypnotize someone's soul.

The ugly kisser spoke:

"***Heil Me!***"

The horrid organism oozed into the drain.

It disappeared, leaving behind a sticky trail that spiraled on the floor. It was the two worms, combined into one, that had earlier been in Link's awful dream.

Link and Dink had been helped to their feet, and along with Tim, Todd, and Annie Tester, stood in shock and disbelief.

Head Chef Grumbel had already vacated the premises, taking the gold-framed uniform and the contents of the *shammes* from the "trophy room."

The questions that remained on the minds of the former prisoners and their rescuers:

What was the awful aberrance that had exited Coffery's body and just snaked out of the room?

And, would *it* be back?

Chapter 30

The Tender twins were in their bedroom the night of the dramatic rescue of the Playlen twins. Sleeping for the boys was becoming a difficult task.

All four pieces of the famed T&P club and Miss Tester had been dubbed Saint Petersburg heroes. Head Chef Grumbel had been given his tribute posthumously.

After experiencing the entire scene of the shooting of Eve; Deacon's failed attempt at firing on himself, severing his right thumb and forefinger in the process; the SS's eventual success at death by way of poisoning; and the awful creature that exited *Kommandant* Coffery's corpse, Tim just knew that he was going to have a *doozie* of a nightmare.

"Todd, are you asleep?" Tim's brother didn't answer. "Todd! Todd!" Still, not a peep. "He must've finally nodded off."

About a half an hour later, the younger twin's eyelids grudgingly closed.

"Oh, great! I'm floating again and there's Todd and Tim...me...snoozing in their beds.

The Tender boys didn't have bunkbeds like the Playlens; they liked twin racks, and Todd's was resting against the west wall, while Tim's was hugging the east wall.

"At least this time," Tim Tender pointed downward, "there's no tombstones over our heads."

Before he could think *bad dream*, Tim was away from the safe bounds of his bedroom, and family, standing in front of a place that he did not recognize...a place that felt and looked dreadful. It was *just* an evil emotion that seemed to move right through him.

There was a tall gate with a phrase written across the top, connected on either side to a large striped pole. He was being pushed closer—by what he had no idea. The wrought iron sign read, in a language other than American:

WARHEIT MACHT FREI.

Out of nowhere, the phrase turned into English:

WORK SETS YOU FREE. Just as quickly the curious slogan swerved back to its original tongue. Tim couldn't understand, maybe he didn't want to.

The next thing that he observed initially frightened him: a vision of a man—substantially built—walking by many multi-level, reddish-orange brick buildings toward Tim from the other side of the gate. When the image got closer, Tim Tender knew the face.

It was Head Chef Grumbel.

The chef wasn't smiling, but he was waving to Tim with his left hand, the one he had lost, along with his wrist and forearm, in the auto tragedy in St. Petersburg. The chef wanted his young friend to come through the entrance. Tim hesitated—but for a single second had a good sensation—it didn't last. The very moment that he passed through the barrier, **desperation**, **loneliness**, **horror**, and **sorrow** reached deep into the deepest region of his soul.

"Welcome, Timothy," the spirit said grabbing the young boy's arm, "this was my home-away-from-home for four years; of course, nothing like the restful Suwannee Hotel back in Florida. This is a concentration camp. Not at all like the Nazi POW camp you saw at the Park Theater. Forget about *Stalag 17*.

"I don't understand," Tim followed his guide farther into the yard.

"I am here to teach you," Tim's companion answered. "As you know I was originally from Poland, but my real name is not Grumbel. That's Glinda's name that I took when we married, hoping to live our lives in peaceful obscurity. My actual name is Casimir Croclaw."

Tim thought about part of the phrase that Mrs. Grumbel had written on Chef Grumbel's headstone at the Cemetery Hill Graveyard in St. Petersburg.....*Just the same, you have my name*....Now he understood.

"This is not my hometown, Cracow; the area around here used to be a nice place to live. The civilians were either expelled or sent to work camps. Don't worry, I will protect you."

"From what?" Tim noticed that Mr. Croclaw, alias Chef Grumbel, was wearing the striped uniform—with red triangle over the number "756"—that had previously been hanging in Coffery's "trophy room."

"Hurry, Timothy, the orchestra is just about to start playing."

Tim Tender was next walking beside Casimir Croclaw over wooden railroad trestles that were between metal railways. There were dark grey and black rocks and green and yellow weeds among each wood beam that they stepped over. The tracks led to another reddish-orange brick building with a semi-circular opening that had a room with many windows and a roof in the same shape as the Tin Woodsman's hat in the *Wizard Of Oz*. Tim felt that he wasn't in Florida anymore.

Through the gap, Tim noticed a fence with lots of barbed-wire, electrical spools, and lantern-style lamps. The two companions from different dimensions advanced slowly into the train station entrance and halted on a dock. There were many German soldiers standing and puffing cigarettes, talking and laughing with one another. The smoke left the cigs in a trail that twisted like one a rattlesnake leaves behind after shifting through a barren desert. Tim couldn't understand what they were saying or joking about but sensed that they were waiting for someone or something to arrive at the station. The "sick sticks"—Mom Tender's label for cigarettes since Grandpa Tender had died—were either being flicked off the dock onto the train tracks or squashed on the polished concrete of the raised platform by the heavy black boots that each SS was wearing.

Croclaw pointed toward the northwest. Tim was able to see a different kind of thick haze, which blew up in large, round puffs from the stack of a train engine that seemed far away, chugging its course toward the station. The huge iron machine looked blurry and traveled in a wet mirage caused by the extreme heat that seemed to be present in Tim's fantasy? He thought maybe this could be a version of the Hell that he had learned about in Sunday School at Fifth Avenue Baptist—he hoped not.

"Mr. Croclaw, what day is it? What week? What year?" Tim was confused. "I've lost track of time."

The prison philharmonic began to play as the train entered the grounds.

"Timothy, the symphony members are performing the opera *Lohengrin*, the 'libretto' written by the German composer, Richard Wagner—one of the camp *kommandant's* favorite composers," Casimir Croclaw said, ignoring Tim's questions, "also, sacred 'cantatas' by Johann Sebastian Bach can, on occasion, be heard coming from the camp's loud speakers."

The boxcar cattle doors behind the foreign "iron horse" opened, and thousands of people in outfits—some striped, some not—disembarked. They were being shoved in every direction by the butts or bayonets of rifles wielded by the SS. There were old men and women, middle-aged women and men, young men and women, and children—all ages, female and male. Tim also noticed lots of luggage that the some of the people had brought being snatched from them and loaded onto railway-station carts. The wagons of baggage then disappeared.

Young Tender saw that many of the new arrivals seemed to have numbers and triangles in the same spot as his guide's. But there were other colors as well as red: greens... blacks...pinks...violets...but the yellows in the shape of stars, stars with six instead of five points that were under red triangles, were the most abundant—by far.

"Mr. Tender, some of these people are experiencing this new lifestyle for the first time, while others are here transferred from similar camps. The camp personnel uses the different colors to distinguish each kind of prisoner," Tim's *spirit teacher* said pointing at the new recruits. "REDS are political, like myself; GREENS are for real evildoers such as murderers and muggers; BLACKS are for idle ones that won't work; PINKS are for those of the same sex with a longing for one another; VIOLETS are for the devoutly religious; and, finally, YELLOWS, the Star-of-David yellows overshadowed by the red triangles, are for the JUDEN, the Jews, the truly-hated race."

Casimir told Tim that there was also a Soviet group but they wore no color—he didn't know the reason. "Timothy, multiple colors can be shown by a single prisoner if he or she fits several categories. I've heard of a captive in Seven Block, the one next to the swimming pool, that the guards have nicknamed *The Rainbow.*

A man dressed in a long white lab coat and wearing a white glove on his right hand only was the next *thing* that came to Tim's attention. The man was making selections from the massive crowd of humans—sending some to the left, some to the right, separating people that seemed to be attached to each other. Severe sobbing from men, women, and children alike was the result of these random choices. Some of those chosen were being led away from the prison barracks. As they were leaving, the orchestra was forced to achieve a crowning crescendo in its music.

Tim Tender began to feel that he was in the process of receiving an eerie education that Miss Annie Tester, superb teacher that she was, could never impart from the unmolested confines of her classroom at Lakeside Elementary.

"Timothy, the overseers in the camp are often Jews wearing the green triangles, and they treat their own kind as badly, sometimes worse, than the SS that direct them. The *kommandant* picked these criminals instead of the red triangles," Croclaw put his finger on his coat's triangle, "because he felt they would be more dependable, only looking after their own interests, instead of worrying about political integrity. Unfortunately, with the *greens* in charge—not the *reds*—the conditions are barely bearable."

But, Croclaw also cautioned about the SS guards that lived to see the prisoners suffer. They were always dreaming up fresh forms of mental and physical torture....This perverted pleasure seemed to be the reason that these *repulsive reprobates*—a term Casimir whispered—got out of bed in the morning. He said that even after his eventual escape on June 27, 1944; even after all the years away from this inhumane existence; and even though he was already dead, he felt that the guards—the savage ones—could still reach into his heart, pull it out...stretch...squash...and shatter it.

Unhappily, Casimir Croclaw did not survive St. Petersburg, a place on the other side of the world from this place—a community where he thought safety would be his until he died peacefully in his sleep from old age problems.

"Young Tender," Casimir continued, gently putting a hand on his charge's shoulder, "other types of guards stay in the SS barracks—some are there just to do a job, a by-the-book job, where the prisoners are just objects to be managed. They form the bulk of the security force; they are also the ones that allow the Jewish *traitors* to do their dirty work. Another, and final kind are the 'blessed few'; ones who actually have mercy as a part of their nature and feel the suffering, the humiliation, the sadness of their fellow man. Only, their numbers are too small to make an impact."

Casimir told Tim that the "crazy guards" made life terrifying almost every second of the day and night; Croclaw said it had been so for him since he arrived on June 14, 1940, until his eventual escape.

"Once, one of the sadistic guards paraded myself and other men from our block, Fourteen Block, to shower detail during the dead of winter. Our prison residence was next to the Camp Bordello, where the women there were the only camp callers allowed to leave in the morning after their one- night stands. After pushing us passed the Nazi pleasure palace, the guard assembled us in the undressing chamber, which began to fill with steam that was seeping over from the hot water spilling down from the shower heads. The SS scum made us open the windows while disrobing, the whole time shouting obscenities. He then chased us into the water now having been reversed to almost ice cubes and forced the men to stand under it for what seemed like an eternity. Our evil escort's final pleasure was to watch with contempt while the human icicles tried to towel off and redress."

Mr. Croclaw said that this act of indecency was child's play compared to the Nazi cleansing solution that was, at a later time, to pour down mercilessly out of the shower heads.

Until the recent tragedies in St. Petersburg, Tim Tender had always thought that people were people, and humans should love each other and help one another. But, in this place in his dream and in the city where he was in reality sleeping next to Todd, he hoped, Tim was learning harsh lessons. Lessons that he would never forget.

Casimir Croclaw and Tim Tender instantly appeared inside one of the many structures that all looked the same from the outside: light-and-dark brown buildings with large doors that opened on either end that reminded Tim of long, skinny barns.

The beds in the barracks didn't resemble Tim's comfy twin bed at *2016 25th Street South* in his hometown....These were stalls made out of rigid wood compressed between brick walls, with barely enough room to toss and turn. Also, there was straw or hay and a small grey blanket in each bunk.

There were as many rats as people; the rodents were crawling to every point of the compass.

"Timothy, we are now in Twenty-two Block, which is next to the SS hospital. There is a ceremony taking place at the north end of the barracks. In reality, the items that you will see being used in this 'celebration of life' would not be available in this awful place. I am showing you what these block members are imagining, trying, if only briefly, to take their minds, if not their bodies, away from here. Let's get closer." The two companions moved respectfully.

A teenaged boy was the focus of the observance by the others attending. He was wearing a *yarmulke*, the skull cap, and a beautiful shawl that had fringes at the bottom of its corners—mostly white, a few blue. The young man was removing the velvet cover from a scroll that had three gold adornments: a crown, a breastplate, and a bell. The new teenager began to read from the roll of parchment, which Casimir said was the *TORAH,* the "Written Law," believed by the Orthodox Jew to have been directly communicated by God to Moses on Mt. Sinai. Tim's guide told him that the boy was reading from the first book, one of five of the Hebrew scriptures.

After his reading, the young man led the group in prayer. The happy event, even in the face of such dire death and destruction, was the thirteen-year old boy's *bar mitzvah*—his initial adult act. Tim also noticed a young girl that was wearing the same type of shawl and *yarmulke* as the young boy. "Timothy, she is waiting to perform the same ceremony, which, in her case, is called a *bat mitzvah*. The boy and girl are twins.

"Timothy," Croclaw held his arms out, "Twenty-two Block is not a synagogue by the distance of anyone's imagination but it will suffice. This sort of thing helps to keep minds and faiths intact."

The two observers observed a prayer spoken that the new inductees into adulthood would be able to develop their grown-up qualities. Tim said his own prayer for their success.

The boy and the girl both vowed *strength*, *courage*, and *honesty*. Tim told Casimir that the two teenagers reminded him of Rod and Kim, his brother and sister.

"Timothy, this next barracks is nicknamed 'The Zoo.'" The room was overflowing with children, some as young as five, most the age of eight, nine, or ten, others older. Even though the boys were wearing bright white pantaloons and starched shirts and the girls looked lovely in their beautiful silk dresses, they had expressions of depression on their scrubbed-clean faces. Tim noticed that this shelter was almost spotless, unlike the one that he had just vacated.

"Mr. Croclaw, are these children imagining how clean this barracks is?...and being dressed this way?" Tim's puzzlement was showing deeply on his face.

"No, this is as you see it. Timothy, I'm going to leave you alone here; I'll catch up to you later." Croclaw quickly vanished.

When he got closer, young Tender saw that all the kids were lookalikes...identical twins...duplicate versions of one another. He slowly moved in behind a duo of boys who immediately performed similar 180-degree turns and stared into Tim's eyes—it was Link and Dink. They were outfitted just like the other boys in the barracks. But, each Playlen had hundreds of hypodermic needles sticking out of every inch of his body. Teardrops were streaming down their faces, coming down furiously like water flying out of a fire hydrant opened full-throttle on a steamy summer day for kids on endless blocks in Brooklyn, Queens, and the Bronx. Dink and Link weren't husky, they were skinny, dangerously skinny— at least twice as skinny as Tim. Tender blinked his eyes in disbelief and the Playlen twins departed.

"Link. Dink. Where did you go? Come back."

Suddenly, he was in another part of the camp and spotted his own brother dressed in ragged, filthy clothing. Todd was bent over, holding his stomach; then, he lifted up; surged forward toward a small chamber; opened the door; and fell butt-first onto a dirty oval seat with the middle missing that covered a huge hole in the ground. The words *das Badezimmer* were written over the door, and the stench in this area of Tim's fantasy was starting to make him feel ill. His twin disappeared and reappeared at the identical spot where Tim had first seen him. The same scene took place—over and over. Tim Tender was finally able to reach for Todd Tender to help him, but his brother, this time, dissolved completely.

"Todd, Todd, come back, where did you go? What is happening? Are Link and Dink with you? Do you see Chef Grumbel?"

Tim said in desperation, trying to find someone he knew to explain this awful state of dream sequences.

In the next instant, he was back in "The Zoo" and one of the pretty, yellow-haired, blue-eyed girls, sitting beside an exact physical match of herself, spoke: "Is 'Uncle' Mengele coming soon? Is he bringing more candy? My sister and I like it better when he brings goodies instead of X-rays, injections, and blood tests."

The door of the barn flew open, and an image of a heavyset woman with an unattractive face and dark, angry eyes stood in the doorway. She was dressed almost entirely in black.

"*Wo ist meine Sohn, Josef?*" the large woman yelled. "He spends all his time with you strange ones; he never has time for his mother. I need him to cheer me up, as only he can do." As she left, she kicked a young boy in the back and said she was going to look for *Josef* in building "P," which, according to her, was one of his best-loved buildings.

The same door that the old peasant woman departed through opened for a second time, and the man in the white lab coat and single white glove, once again, became the focus of Tim's range of sight. Tender assumed that he was some kind of doctor. Or was this a Halloween costume? The figure had a smile, a big smile, on his kisser and said, "Good day, my 'chosen ones,' it is time for more fun. As your 'angel of mercy,' I will treat you, no trick, to more exciting experiments. You should be proud to take part in such important study. We must go. Block Fifteen is being readied." In a flash, the room was emptied.

Young Tender was dispatched through space-and-dream-time to a building with the number Ten labeled on it. He wasn't inside Fifteen Block with the other twins; he was outside in a courtyard between Ten Block and Eleven Block.

Casimir Croclaw rejoined his dazed student in this place and pointed toward a wall, a black wall surrounded by a brick wall, at the far end of the square.

"Timothy, it is now November 11, 1941, and this is an execution area called 'The Black Wall of Death,' a term that every prisoner in camp is familiar with. Watch."

Tim observed in horror as a prisoner was put to death with a small-calibre weapon, shot in the back of the neck. Tim wanted to vomit but couldn't—he told Croclaw to stop the terror, but Casimir wouldn't....This dreadful page of history, of which there existed millions of similar pages, took the lives, in the same deadly manner, of 150 more of Casimir Croclaw's countrymen.

"Mr. Croclaw, I want to go home and be with my family and friends."

"Sorry, Timothy, but other teachings are critical; there is much more that you need to *see, hear, smell, feel,* and *touch*."

Tim needed to see the relentless death and destruction; he needed to hear the awful cries of pain and suffering; he needed to smell the stink of burning flesh and the reek of bodies—dead for days and weeks, piled atop each other like pick-up sticks; he needed to feel the loneliness of families and friends torn apart, never again to come in contact with one another; and, finally, he needed to touch his heart and pray that this terrible case of *man's inhumanity to man* would never ever happen again.

Tim Tender woke within his bad dream—his face stuffed in a filthy pillow that had a urine smell worse than any left from a week's worth of baby Everett's dirty diapers fermenting in the diaper bin.

The bed, with straw over the wood slats, felt harder and smelled worse than resting on the floor of the back porch of his home near the punk trees that always cast such an awful odor.

"You're in the stall that was formerly *my* teenage son's. He died after contracting *cholera*, for which he received no treatment. I desperately tried to get the guards to do something for him. They never did." Casimir also told Tim that he had had four daughters and a wife—not Glinda, who was his second wife—that had been sent to the women's barracks the day the whole family arrived at the camp. One week later they were all dead.

"My family came here after we were taken from our house in Cluj, Romania. It was a new home that we had moved to from Cracow. We were told by the Germans that we were going to a labor camp in central Hungary; but, when the train finally came to a stop after two days of traveling, we knew, even before departing the cattle car, that Hungary was not the destination. Instead, the Croclaw family was introduced to one of Hitler's many death camps." Casimir told Tim that he was the only survivor of his kindred that made it out of the hell hole.

Casimir Croclaw informed Tim that, in a while, he was going to take him on a trip, a short trip, to the main camp's *sister* camp over by the train station. Somehow Tim knew that this would not be an excursion the type of the annual Tender vacation getaway to the beach of Gulfport. How Tim wished that he was there right now.

"Why don't you reflect on those Gulfport trips awhile, Tim."

"Mr. Croclaw, how did you know what I was think...?"

Casimir disappeared.

Tim started to feel awful about the fact that he and Todd would always complain to their dad, after five or six or seven years straight of staying at the same small motel located on the same side street directly north of the sandy shore of the small town west of St. Petersburg. The boys had always wanted just once for the yearly respite to take place somewhere, anywhere else.

Dad Tender had moved from Towanda, Pennsylvania, to Saint Petersburg, Florida. Eventually, he met Mom Tender at Aunt Martha's Candy Shop downtown on 242 1st Avenue North, where she was working at the time.

Later, he began to feel the need not to stray too far from home. By moving to the Sunshine State, Tim and Todd's dad obtained everything he needed family-wise, weather-wise, and job-wise.

In his concentration-camp crash course, Tim was realizing that there existed worse places—by light years— than Gulfport, and when he saw his dad again, Tim would make a point of telling him how he enjoyed the yearly journey to the salty water of Boca Ciega Bay.

Tim started to daydream in his nightmare. He thought about when he and Todd would go, after a day on the beach of swimming and sunbathing and badmintoning and barbecuing, to the A&W Root Beer Stand on Shore Boulevard in Gulfport.

The place had a pocket billiard's table. The twins loved to play pool; that is, after the teenagers got done using the table. Even though they never took down a score, if they had kept track, after one hundred games, it would probably be fifty-one wins and forty-nine losses for Todd and just the opposite for Tim. Todd was four minutes older and had a little more experience.

The boys usually played *eight ball* or *straight pool* unless Rod honored them with his presence—which he did if none of his buddies were around...after all, he had his *rep* to keep up. Together, the trio of Tenders would usually play three-way *elimination* or as Rod called it: *cutthroat*. Of course, when he was in one of his mean moods, Rod would only let one of the twins share his game while the other sat and watched. The teenage Tender never lost to either of his younger brothers. Roddy was too talented and too vain when it came to pocket pool or poker, his two favorite games of challenge. Once, when he was on a hot streak, Rod sank 150 balls in a row, calling each hole. He would've drained many more, but as he was stroking the cue ball for the 151st time, a curvy redhead walked in the A&W and fouled-up his focus.

Tim pondered on something that Rod had once told him but not Todd about:

Rod Tender one day hoped to share a rack with the great William "Willie" Mosconi. Although Rudolf Wanderone, Jr., better known as "Minnesota Fats," would state otherwise, Rod felt Mosconi was the *best*. After all, since 1941 Willie had been world champ many times over. He was a real *pro*.

Rod Tender knew a lot about billiards, its history and personalities, and said that Fats was just a blowhard—a "spinner of tales." The "Fatman" even claimed to have actually played a game with Adolf Hitler.

The Tender teen said that Wanderone had been born in Manhattan and always stated to anyone who would listen: "The pool table was my crib." Rod told his brothers that Fats would travel the USA in his Cadillac looking for action at the tables and "tomatoes" (his flattering word for women); that is, until he married his wife, Evelyn, in 1941. That ceremony immediately squeezed all the juice out of his "tomato" hunt. Rod told the twins that even though he had to admit that "Minnesota" was a remarkable pool player, he was a hustler searching for suckers and would never be as great as "Willie," the *billiard king*.

Out of his trance, young Tender next found himself, along with Casimir, in a room with many washtubs lined up in rows, evenly-spaced from one to the next. These tubs reminded him of the kind that he and Todd used to clean Frisky in—their runaway mutt. Only these were wooden with two gold-metal strips surrounding each. The wood looked the same as the dark-and-light lumber of the buildings where the prisoners were housed. The space appeared empty except for Tim and his ghostly host.

"Mr. Croclaw, there doesn't seem to be anyone here."

"Timothy, move closer to the barrels."

As he stared inside the tubs, Tim discovered one of the most appalling scenes he'd ever been exposed to: liquid filled almost to the top edge and babies—short...long... wide...thin babies—under the water. Babies with dark, red, light, or no hair. Babies that were once cute or once plain but all adorable. But now, these precious little ones were ugly because murder is never pretty. Tim could not believe what his eyes were showing him. These innocent, tiny human beings had been drowned to death.

But why?

"There is no explanation for this, Timothy, just blind hatred, and stupidity, which I will never understand."

In the next moment, the mother of each small infant appeared over her baby's *drowning pool*. Some of the women were weeping uncontrollably with salty-liquid covering every inch of their faces. Some were standing silently with only trickles of tears evident. Some were just staring without visible emotion at *those* they carried inside them for so long, only to have their loved ones taken away in scarcely more time than it takes to blink. And, some seemed as if they had been pushed to a trance-like state, never to return from wherever it was that their minds were lost.

"There aren't any men in this area of the *sister* camp," Casimir told Tim as he pulled the boy away from the tubs, "only women and children. And after already being separated from their husbands, fathers, uncles, or brothers, now the wives, daughters, nieces, or sisters have been permanently detached from their beloved newborns—but only in this world."

"Mr. Croclaw, the ones responsible for such atrocities must have come from a species far below even the insect kingdom."

Casimir Croclaw did not disagree.

Tim Tender began to get, in his nose, a hint of a gas-like smell different from the odor that wafts out of a cooking stove that has one of its handles turned to low, medium, or high while the pilot light is out. This aroma reminded him of almonds. Strange.

"This is a *chamber of horrors*," the ghostly guide said, "but not like the fun-filled *chamber of scares* they have every year at the Lakeside Halloween Carnival. This one is the real thing."

The duo of dream merchants were standing in a dark, dank concrete basement staring at stairs that lead to the upper level of the building.

Tim could hear shuffling going on upstairs and was informed that hair was being shaved from the newly-chosen prisoners; prisoners who thought they were in this place to be deloused for the removal of parasites from their bodies. This process was to be completed before herding them down the long set of corkscrew stairs to the lower level, where Tender and Croclaw were waiting for Tim to view his next horrifying homework assignment.

Casimir said, at this point, this parade of humans was not like cattle being pushed and prodded and pulled into an involuntary stampede; instead, these detainees, not really knowing where they were going, were mostly calm and completely clueless to their actual fate.

Finally, men, women, and children—all ages, all sizes...tall, short, mostly thin, painfully thin—filed down the steps. Most were wearing serene looks on their faces, although, a few seemed to sense evil in the air. For them, the *Sonderkommando*—earmarked teams of Jewish captives—to soothe the troublemakers and keep them from getting the rest riled-up.

Tim began to feel that more than disinfection was involved here.

The doors opened to a room on the northwest side of the building and young Tender saw rows and rows and rows of shower heads—they seemed to go on forever. The hostages were shoved into the showers by SS guards that yelled: *"Schnell! Schnell! Schnell!"* The huge doors were closed and bolted.

Then, the guards brought out small metal cans labeled, **Cyclon B Pellets**, and disappeared with them. Tim began to hear screaming worse than any he had ever heard and louder than any thunder he had ever experienced.

Some time passed; then, it became deadly silent. The doors were unlocked and immediately an awful, jarring pungency—that familiar smell of nuts—hit Tender directly in the face.

Croclaw led him into the room, where the humans that had just been walking and talking were now lying motionless on the concrete carpet of the *killing stalls*. Their fingers, toes, lips, and ears had all turned dark blue.

Tim began to cry.

He felt that he couldn't stand much more exposure to the constant pain and suffering, but Casimir was relentless and determined to show him more.

Instantly, the *Sonderkommando* began to drag out the dead and pile the corpses into large elevators for transport to the ground level.

"Timothy, the prisoners will now be checked for expensive fillings in their mouths."

The large freight elevator doors shut tight, and Tim Tender was on the move once again.

The heat was unbearable....Tim had learned at Fifth Avenue Baptist about how hot it was supposed to be in Hell but couldn't imagine a single degree hotter than what he was presently experiencing.

He was standing beneath a sign that Casimir translated: "Timothy, it says, **'Crematory and Gas Chamber 2.'**" It was located on the top level of the same structure of his basement assignment. "There are five ovens, Timothy, each with three openings, where many prisoners are reduced to ashes like those that come from every lighted Lucky Strike or Pall Mall that has ever been smoked," Casimir said holding an imaginary cigarette.

But, Tim didn't stay in this place long. He was conveyed to a forest area with leafless, charred trees and large open pits that were empty except for a thick, black dust that covered the entire area of the tremendous cavities. Instantly, a large swell of smoke like a magician uses to appear out-of-nowhere, flashed before Tim's eyes. After the smoke cleared, there were bodies.

"Mr. Croclaw! Mr. Croclaw! those are some of the people I saw in the showers."

"Yes, Timothy, the 'death showers.'"

The bodies were being pushed into the pits onto the top of dark figures barely recognizable as once being humankind. The fresh corpses were set on fire, and, again, fumes emerged and blew tall through the trees toward the overcast sky.

Tim recognized the crackling sound of fire as the identical one that screamed forth out every bonfire ever built at Camp Spartan in St. Petersburg. But the smell, this putrid stench of burning flesh, had never been evident back home except in this dreadful dream.

There were many SS soldiers standing shirtless—the leg bottoms of their pants stuffed into scuffed black boots. Some of them had hats, others hatless—all drinking from bottles of German beer.

"This is an enjoyment for most of the guards, but a few are drinking not only to battle the tremendous heat caused by the incineration, but also to get drunk, as drunk as possible. *They know that it is the only way to handle the extermination, enforced by their superiors, of persons of their own race...the human race,*" Croclaw told Tender. A sad expression came over Casimir's face. Tim had a look of shock and disbelief and he was also saddened.

The next stopover on Tim's Polish-countryside tour was the office of the camp chief, *Kommandant* Hiss. Hiss's quarters were located between the SS Guardhouse and Block One of the prisoners' barracks.

The *Kommandant* was seated—in a chair that seemed to overshadow him—behind a desk, bordered by the black, red, and yellow German flag on one end and the Nazi flag on the other. He was talking to a tall and muscular man with hair as yellow as a lemon peel.

This man was standing at attention in front of the prison leader. The figure had his back toward the area of the room where Casimir and Tim were floating and observing. The one thing that Tim immediately noticed about the upright SS was the scar that reached around the left side of his face, which at the moment, was all that Tender could see. Tim felt that the facial flaw seemed, in an ugly way, familiar.

Directly over the *kommandant's* head, on the wall, was a black velvet painting of Adolf Hitler. In the picture, *Der Fuehrer* had his mouth wide open flashing bright white teeth in a sort of blood-sucking, vampire position—without the famed dual points. And, eyes as evil-looking as any young Tender had ever witnessed.

In the next moment, the two SS soldiers began to converse in an East German tongue. Casimir interpreted:

"Here," the *kommandant* handed some papers to the other SS figure, "you must read the orders from the *Reichsfuhrer SS* about his program, *Lebensborn*, which will begin in our camp," Hiss said. "I have chosen you to be my deputy and have appointed, in writing, your control of the camp while I am attending a meeting with *RFSS* Himmler in Berlin about the removal of Camp *Sachsenhausen's Kommandant.*"

"You mean Loritz?" the dutiful soldier returned, accepting the orders.

"Yes, he had already been booted out of *Dachau* because he cared little about his own prison. Himmler said that he recently visited *Dachau*, and the prisoners did not even take off their caps," he pointed at his own Nazi hat, "in his presence. Nor did they even do the simplest gestures, like saluting Heinrich, a superior officer."

"Is it possible that you will transferring to *Dachau* to correct things?"

"Possibly, possibly...which is why you must take this opportunity that I am gifting you and turn it into a success. Then I can make a recommendation to Himmler on your part to take over the reins of your own barracks."

"*Heil*, Hiss! I will do anything you ask." The newly-appointed assistant clicked his boots together and raised his right arm toward the Nazi flag.

"First, it will be your responsibility to find strong Aryan women, specifically handpicked under the guidelines of the *Lebensborn* program. They will bear the children of our top SS soldiers. The children born from these exceptional unions will be raised in the SS tradition. The families will be able to fill the void left in the eastern areas of Poland and the Soviet Union with powerful German personalities. It will be mergers made in Heaven, do you not agree?"

"Absolutely, *Herr Kommandant*!" Another SS movement was performed with precision by the blonde soldier.

"Secondly, in my absence, with any means at your disposal, you must make sure that the camp remains controllable. Two days after my departure, the inspector of concentration camps will pay you an unannounced visit, expecting to discover inefficiencies in the temporary command."

"Unannounced?"

"Yes, it is supposed to be a surprise inspection to see if I have properly trained those under my charge. Your training has gone well so far, which is why I am assigning you the post," Hiss said. "What Himmler doesn't know is that I have true compatriots at his headquarters who inform me of his every move."

"I will do everything as we previously discussed, *Herr* Hiss," the *kommandant's* new second returned. "The chosen prisoners will be properly detained, disciplined, and disposed of in full view of the examiner. I will also continue to assist and oversee as many of Dr. Mengele's examinations as time will permit."

"Wonderful, I will leave with clear conscience knowing that I have made the *right* choice. By the way, I'm missing my personally-signed copy of *Mein Kampf*. Have you seen it?"

"N...no," the adjunct moved his head as if searching for the book, "bu...but, I wi...ll make it my specific struggle to locate it and return it to your desk."

Then, the *kommandant* vanished into thin air and the SS deputy moved around the chief's desk and spoke to himself: "I think I'll try out *my* new chair." He reached into his satchel and pulled out the lost *Mein Kampf* and put it on his lap.

Then Tim Tender fixed on the dark eyes of the new assistant *kommandant,* the pupils of which seemed to suddenly burn an unbroken path into young Tender's eyes.

"**Mr. Croclaw**! he's seen us; he's noticed we're watching him; he stared right at me." Suddenly, Tim focused on the entire face of the SS and centered in on his scar—a scar that began just below his right eye; continued up and over the bridge of his nose; curved down; and ended below his left jaw.

There was no mistake.

It was Coffery—the facial disfigurement was one-of-a-kind.

"It's Coffery! It's Coffery! **Chef Grumbel, look!**"

"Yes, Timothy, it's the Archenemy, Principal Deacon Coffery, better known here as the 'Serpent' for his work with prisoners using methods only a demon would be proud of. He recognized me in St. Petersburg, as I most assuredly did him. Before Glinda and I could get to the authorities, the auto accident of which you are painfully aware sealed my fate.

"But don't fear; he's just an image here. He can't see, hear, or hurt you," Casimir said and then whispered to himself, "I hope and pray."

Casimir Croclaw told Tim Tender that he was now going to leave him; that, with the exception of one last stop, this short life lesson on existence in a concentration camp was finished.

He also related to his young student that they would always be *dear* friends and possibly meet again sometime in the future.

Before he could comprehend the terrifying vision of Coffery as the "SS Serpent" with his deep black eyes and hair the color of the *yellow* in Tim's old Crayola box, young Tender was whisked away to a room that had to be some sort of a medical ward.

Tim was in a place, this time without Casimir, with tons of laboratory equipment: microscopes; glass containers with glass tubing stretching outward; scalpels—twinkling from light bouncing off the razor-sharp blades; tables—long tables that looked like the dissecting counters that Miss Tester used in her Science classes; and *Bunsen* burners, armies of them.

Thanks to Annie Tester, Tim knew that these burners had been invented by Robert Wilhelm Bunsen, a German scientist and professor at Heildelberg in the Nineteenth Century. The invention was supposed to be used for enhancing research projects—and for the *betterment* of mankind.

Tender also noticed orangish-colored double doors on the far end of the room from where he was floating. The doors had some sort of locks hanging from the handles. Tim wondered what could be so important that it had to be secured in such a manner.

In a flash, twins, the "identical" ones, appeared on the table-tops with needles, attached to tubes, sticking out of their arms. Blood, a sea of blood, was spraying everywhere—hitting the walls...the floor...the ceiling—like an abstract artist releasing red paint from his brush onto a giant canvas.

Tim then saw the man that he had previously seen in two other locations, the train station and the "zoo" barracks. He was wearing the lab coat and a glove over each arm. The medical cloak, because of the blood lost from his young patients, was as red as it was white. He was laughing and had a depraved, excited gaze on his face that reminded Tim of the fanatical doctor in Mary Shelley's marvelous novel of terror, *Frankenstein.* There must have been twenty-five pairs of twins on the tables, and they were all screaming in unison:

"Please, 'Uncle' Mengele, stop, stop; we don't like these experiments anymore, they are not fun."

With that, Tim began to move towards the double doors. As he approached, the dual, rusty metal portals flew open.

A strong suction pulled Tender in. Inside there were four gooseneck lanterns, equally-spaced apart, one each hanging over a large glass tank that held a salty-looking liquid. The containers had something in them bobbing back-and-forth, up-and-down.

When he got close enough to see the contents of the clear receptacles, Tim couldn't believe the horrifying sight: it was the heads, just the heads, of all four members of the famed T&P club.

Crash!—The faces broke out of the huge beakers, glass flew everywhere, and opaque fluid *waterfalled* to the floor. Instantly, wooden plaques with the mugs of Todd, Tim, Link, and Dink were fastened to the back wall like stuffed animals.

Tim finally woke up and his entire twin bed was wet. His whole body was covered with sweat. Young Tim felt that he had just experienced the worst *Tender nightmare* of his life.

But what was only a terrible dream for him was a reality for eleven million human beings—six million Jews—who died without mercy. And, numberless others were scarred for life as a result of the insanity, prompted by a single maniacal man.

Tim felt drained of all emotion and was relieved that Deacon Coffery and Eve Brown had disappeared from the face of the earth; therefore, unable to execute more death and destruction in *his* St. Petersburg, or anywhere else.

Tim could hear his twin brother, Todd, snoring solidly and was happy to be home safe. But, he felt that he would never get over the awful atrocities that he had witnessed—only a small portion of—in the countryside of Poland.

Epilogue

Mr. and Mrs. Deacon Coffery...alias...*Kommandant and Frau Coffery*...died on that day, November 2, 1954, over a year ago. Cowardly deaths.

The recovered copy of *Mein Kampf* that the Saint Petersburg *kommandant* claimed had been personally signed by the author to him, actually had another name—scribbled out—next to *Kommandant* Coffery's monogram. It was a partial name written in the identical hand of the creator of the Nazi propaganda sheets, both contrary to the writing of Coffery's signature. Curious. The only letters that could be made out were H-o-s; a bullet hole had replaced the rest. The book was later burned.

* * *

It was the end of the year of our Lord, 1955, and the town of St. Petersburg seemed as though it had returned to the tranquil nature that it had enjoyed before the evil principal had shown his Nazi face, and converted his dangerously loyal secretary. Both their bodies had been cremated by the coroner because the funeral director, A. Hister, had to spend a little time in the lockup for selling Granny Hart's body. Deacon's and Eve's ashes were placed in a locked strong box and buried so deep that they could dance in the "Fires of Hell."

Chef Grumbel/Casimir Croclaw was hopefully resting in peace.

Miss Tester changed her feeling about ghosts.Link and Dink Playlen had made a full recoveries; Todd became more cautious; and Tim Tender had not experienced any further nightmares.

One of the worst things that befell the Tender twins was that the Playlen twins had moved to Miami, Florida, a place that their parents felt would be a safer environment in which to finish raising their children. They may have been right.

It was a cold December day. Tim and Todd were on Christmas leave and standing in Mrs. Grumbel's yard, hoping that she would come out and chat with them. She had started talking again.

After the dreadful deeds of the previous year, the only places the twins were allowed to go by themselves was to their new school, Southskid Junior High, and Lakeside Elementary. Adult supervision, usually their parents, was required for any additional adventures. No passing "Go" or stopping at Denington's.

This process would continue for awhile, hopefully not for infinity, the twins trusted. But, even Todd had lost some of his boldness, which had always made him a daredevil.

Mrs. Grumbel had become a nicer person, especially after she had stopped drinking. And, her salary for her Head Custodian's position was doubled by the new principal, Miss Annie Tester. The Tenders wanted to tell the caretaker that they were going to buy the latest Lego Block toys from Webb's City and present them at Christmas, which was on Sunday that year, to the kids of needy cooks—Mrs. Grumbel's favorite charity.

They waited for what seemed like an eternity and, finally, walked up her maplewood steps—made with the previous principal's desk and other pieces of furniture—and knocked on her shiny maplewood door.

No answer.

Very odd.

"Let's go into the schoolhouse and look for her," Tim said as he pointed toward the back door.

"Sounds good," Todd turned and started to walk toward the cement steps, "but first I have to use the bathroom."

They entered the restroom on the first floor at the south end of the building. Instantly, they came to a halt, as if they were each hit with a punch as hard as the one that the champ, Rocky

Marciano, *KO'd* Archie Moore with in their heavyweight bout in 1955. "Oh no, not again!" Tim screamed, "this can't be happening again. Not again."

Todd, with his hands over his mouth, stood silently and stared upward.

A body, neck stretching in a noose, was hanging from the lightpole that attached to the ceiling. It was Head Custodian Grumbel. She had her good hand and the crippled hand tied together behind her back with chicken wire.

"We have to get her down, Todd."

The Tender twins managed to remove her from the rope and place her on the floor.

"I...I'll go...go call the po...police!" Todd said frantically, as he rushed past the urinals.

In a matter of minutes—it seemed—Sheriff Martin Milk and Deputy Jock Juice, John Daniels' and Jack Walker's replacements, were on the scene, and Deputy Juice rushed Mrs. Grumbel to Mound Park Hospital.

Todd and Tim were later credited with saving their friend's life. Modest heroes a second time.

After realizing that Mrs. Grumbel had not committed the previous killings in town, Daniels and Walker actually dried out and took jobs as forest rangers at Mt. Pisgah in the Pennsylvania woods.

Sheriff Martin Milk, along with Tim and Todd, searched the restroom. The lawman found a note underneath one of the flush toilets. It read:

My life without my dear sweetheart amounts to nothing more than a wretched, smelly fart; therefore, from this world I depart...Glenda Grumble.

Neither Tender twin believed a word of the morbid memo. Mrs. Grumbel had been extremely happy and had everything to live for; so, the suicide note was not logical.

Tim asked to see the note: "Sheriff! the signature on here is misspelled; that's not how she spells her name. She spells Glinda with an *i* and Grumbel with *el* not *le*."

Good eye.

Sheriff Milk and the boys continued to explore the lavatory for additional clues.

"Hey, I've found something here in the corner," Todd said as he bent down and picked up a small breast pin, "it has *Klara's Funeral Parlor* hand painted on it."

Also, good eye.

Tim said: "That's A. Hister's place."

Then, Principal Tester entered the room.

"What's going on here?"

The entire situation was explained to the former super teacher, now super principal, who was reassured by the others in the room that Mrs. Grumbel would be alright.

Milk, Tester, Tender, and Tender all piled into the black-and-white squad car and raced toward *The Palatial Palace of Passing*. *It*, like Lakeside Elementary and Lakehood High, rested on the banks of Lake Maggiore. The building of deadly detention had been converted from a once stately mansion that had Russian spires, gargoyles, and helmeted soldiers, each ornate in design, running the length and width of the building. They seemed to be on constant watch.

The top law dog, who had previously radioed-in to his assistant at the hospital to meet him, told the non-officers to remain in the police car until they were given the "sign" that it was safe to enter Klara's. A huge wave from Deputy Jock Juice at the doorway came within minutes of the officers' entry into the deadly world of A. Hister.

The remaining trio rushed out of the *copper* car, ran up the walkway, advanced through the door, proceeded down the hallway, and followed Juice into a room that was full of caskets.

Coffins were everywhere but there was only one with its lid open, a stone one with intricate decorations, which was where

Sheriff Milk was standing, looking in. The death box was obviously built for a small adult. Another peculiar yet scary sight in the parlor was situated in the southeast corner: two mannequins stuck together—one male, one female—dressed in outfits that sent shivers down the spines of Tim, Todd, and Annie Tester. The dummies were outfitted in the clothes that were on the bodies of *Kommandant* Coffery and his dutiful secretary/wife, Eve, when they perished.

The *CFEO* (Chief Funeral Executive Officer) was inside the small sarcophagus. Most of his flesh had been eaten away and a plastic bag was over his head.

"This is gruesome." Sheriff Milk picked up a note that was lying next to the body. "Everybody keep your distance. The letter reads, 'I hanged Glenda Grumble at dawn and I don't know why; therefore, I can no longer walk the face of the earth. Good-bye, Cruel World. Heil!' It's signed by A. Hister."

Tim was grateful that he didn't view the dead body of the "burial boss"; even though, he had started towards it. But, what Tim Tender did discover, had he shared it with anyone, may have caused the worst feeling of doom yet for the other four living occupants of the "room of caskets": as he backed away from the limestone coffin, one of Tim's white-with-black-label Keds stuck to the concrete floor of the casket chamber.

Timothy told me (the Red Sox fan) years later—as we waited out a five-day snowstorm at a Red Cross haven near the university in Boston that we both haunted—that what he had stepped in was a trail of sticky slime. The muck led toward a drain situated near the ghastly statues of Mr. and

Mrs. Deacon Coffery. A snakelike path, which could have been caused by a worm, Timothy thought.

Timothy Tender never told any past or present Saint Petersburg residents, not even his own twin, about his accidental detection.

Except for myself, his *dear* friend.

The End.

Afterword

...first applied to the attempted extermination of the Jews by Nazi Germany; The systematic killing of, or a program of action intended to destroy, a whole national or ethnic group.

Webster's New College Dictionary—third edition— describes "genocide" with the above definition.

And as most people realize living in places other than caves since 1925—the year the evil *Mein Kampf* was started—Adolf Hitler, *summa cum laude* graduate from Devil University (a hot spot for aspiring Satan worshippers), was the embodiment of the Nazi party.

One of the many prophecies made by Nostradamus, the French physician and astrologer, in the Sixteenth Century, was that a man he labeled *A. Hister* would be considered an anti-Christ. With that prediction, Michel de Nostredame, the actual name of the author of *Centuries*, describing events from the mid-1500s to the end of the world (his best guess: AD 3797), was— tragically—"right on the money."

And, even though the chancellor of the Third Reich has been in the ground over fifty years, his fascist philosophies are still being followed even today. Hence, this manuscript becomes a sort of "warning" asserting that, unfortunately, *Der Fuehrer* still lives in the souls of many—*too many*.

As I am writing this "Afterword" on April 13, 1999 *(Holocaust Remembrance Day)*, sadly, the NATO airstrikes and fighting continue across Yugoslavia and three American soldiers remain captured as POWs. These drastic measures taken to try and curb

Slobodan Milosevic's *take-no prisoners* game plan against the citizens of Albania.

The Serbian leader's tag of "The Butcher of the Balkans" that he proudly secured because of his *ethnic cleansing* is only one clue that, in this author's opinion, Adolf Hitler has yet to "leave the building"—using a saying spawned from the great Elvis Presley's concerts. (I apologize to "The King of Rock 'n' Roll" for using his name in the same sentence as "the leader of death and destruction.")

Sorrowfully, Hitler's slanted ideals, policies, and fanatical attitudes—like the fictional Principal (*alias Kommandant*) Deacon Coffery of the tale that you, the reader, hopefully, have just enjoyed—have remained in the hearts and minds of many a racial lunatic.

The final chapter has yet to be written in the Serb/ Albanian conflict, and the numbers are not as staggering (yet?) as those credited (discredited—a word more appropriate) to others.

Others like the inhumane human (human status very questionable?) being called Pol Pot, former (some say still) head of the Khmer Rouge. The K.R. masking as a movement that overthrew the Cambodian government in 1975. Under Pot's proud leadership, extensive executions, forced labor, and famine killed an approximated three million Cambodians.

There have been many other incidences of "genocide" beyond Hitler's reign of terror—though, he was given credit (again, the term "discredit" crops up) for coining the cancerous phrase.

Another case of holocaust took place during the regime of horror carried-out by dictator Idi Amin after vanquishing President Milton (Apollo) Obote in 1971.

The following disclosures were taken from *The Concise Columbia Encyclopedia*:

Obote was overthrown in 1971 by Maj. Gen. Idi Amin, who inaugurated a period of dictatorial rule that plunged the nation into chaos. He purged the Lango and Acholi tribes, moved against the army, and in 1972 expelled 60,000 non-citizen Asians. By 1977, it is estimated, 300,000 Ugandans had been killed in Amin's reign of terror. Finally, in 1979, an invasion by Tanzanian troops and Ugandan exiles drove out Amin's forces, and Amin fled the country.

Massacring members of a different race is bad enough, but this idiot killed his own countrymen. And who knows how many more Ugandans would have been exterminated, if the fool hadn't been chased out of the homeland.

More horrid examples:

A story by the *Associated Press* on December 13, 1997, retrieved from *America Online* stated that:

ISLAMABAD, Pakistan (AP) - United Nations' human rights investigators have discovered hundreds of bodies in wells and shallow graves in northern Afghanistan, lending credence to Taliban claims of a mass slaughter of its forces, U.N. officials say. The investigators are looking into claims by Uzbek warlord Rashid Dostum that as many as 2,000 Taliban soldiers were massacred during a failed campaign to capture northern Afghanistan in May. Some of the bodies were stuffed in deep wells and others showed signs of torture, said the investigators, who spoke on condition of anonymity.

They probably held back their names in fear of ending up in the same situation as those killed in their report.

And don't think that Americans are above the illogical extermination of humans from other races. The *Concise Columbia Encyclopedia,* licensed by the Columbia University Press listed this example in 1995:

My Lai incident, massacre of civilians in the Vietnam War. On Mar. 16, 1968, U.S. soldiers, led by Lt. William L. Calley, invaded the south Vietnamese hamlet of My Lai, an alleged Viet Cong stronghold, and shot to death 347 unarmed civilians, including women and children. The incident was not made public until 1969. Special army and congressional investigations followed. Five soldiers were court- martialed, and one, Lt. Calley, was convicted (Mar. 29, 1971) and sentenced to life imprisonment. In Sept. a federal court overturned the conviction, and Calley was released.

Vietnam, in the estimation of many, was a war that the United States never should have been involved with in the first place: "I was proud of the youths who opposed the war in Vietnam because they were my babies." This quote by Dr. Benjamin McLane Spock (not the guy with the "pointed ears"), author of the best-selling book, *Common Sense Book of Baby and Child Care*, that was printed in the *Times (*London, 2 May 1988*)*. Dr. Spock was so opposed to the Vietnam conflict that he was arrested, along with 259 others including the poet, Allen Ginsberg, in New York on December 5, 1967.

The writer of *Tender Nightmare* graduated from Lakewood High School in St. Petersburg, Florida, in the late Sixties. Because of a draft lottery the year that I was eligible, the 365 days of the calendar were thrown into a huge metaphoric military helmet, drawn randomly with disorderly conduct, and assigned a number. The day of the year tagged "Number One" would see those individuals born then—lucky or unlucky depending on the point of view of the newest soldiers—taken first into the Armed Services. At what juncture the Selective Service System cut off the induction days, I do not know. Ask any person who went to Vietnam and made it back reasonably intact, and he or she could probably quote the exact day of the year.

The luck of the draw made my twin brother and I two of the *luckiest*—our birthdate didn't turn up until well into the 300s, and millions would've had to have been called before reaching us.

Others weren't so fortunate.

One of my best friends, who lived in our neighborhood, had to experience the atrocities of war; but, he was spared his life. He made it home and is now a successful business owner. An accomplishment that I respect very much. Unfortunately, we've

181

drifted apart (I blame myself) and I hope that we can become acquainted (we'll always be friends) again.

My wife, who was born and raised in Baltimore, Maryland, was friends with two brothers, one two years older than the other. They both went to Vietnam; but, the younger brother was the only one to make it back to the States; the older sibling was killed in a conflict that he should have never been involved with in the first place.

One thing I do know is that these brave soldiers of the Vietnam conflict, as well as, the courageous GIs of the other wars of history, deserve the respect and gratitude of every citizen that lives today in a free environment.

But, these are tragic stories, and war, especially a war like Vietnam—with such controversy surrounding it—where so many civilians were killed, no one knowing if they were communist sympathizers or not, can cause humans to do things they normally wouldn't do.

Philip Caputo, a U.S. author, journalist, and Vietnam veteran, was quoted in *Playboy* magazine (Chicago, Jan. 1982):

There is the guilt all soldiers feel for having broken the taboo against killing, a guilt as old as war itself. Add to this the soldier's sense of shame for having fought in actions that resulted, indirectly or directly, in the deaths of civilians. Then pile on top of that an attitude of social opprobrium, an attitude that made the fighting man feel personally morally responsible for the war, and you get your proverbial walking time bomb.

This statement, in this writer's opinion, holds a huge amount of truth; but, the line should not be crossed where the soldier starts killing anyone, regardless of gender or age, that doesn't have the same image in the mirror as he does, or follow the same beliefs.

Although, unless you were there in Vietnam (or any other place where war was battled), you can never understand the tragedy of the mental, emotional, and physical stress caused by the endless maimings, loss of life, and horror that took place in the Asian jungles.

WAR IS HELL.

But to condone killing in this manner of randomness, some believe, would justify what happened in Hitler's concentration camps.

When I started doing the research on Adolf Hitler's concentration camps, I had no clue as to what I would eventually find. Because of movies, magazines, newspapers, and other forms of communication used to inform the public about historical events, most of us have a shallow idea about what went on during *Der Fuehrer's* "Final Solution" plan.

But through research contained in books written by individuals who actually took part in these events, I learned more, much more than I ever wanted to.

But, it's a story that should never die.

The suffering and humiliation endured by the courageous prisoners and those that were left behind should never be forgotten. It should be remembered as it truly was, one of the most horrible times in the history of the world, so that it may never happen again to such an extent.

Unfortunately, there are still, to this day, groups of followers of Hitler's spirit and ideals who would love to bring about a dangerous reenactment of the World War II's atrocities engineered by *Der Fuehrer*.

This is the continuing tragedy that, hopefully, some day can be cleansed forever.

The Stolen Manuscript: The Dictionary Murders
A Mystery in the Tim Tender Series

A Second Novel

by

Ray E. Spencer

TURN THE PAGE FOR A PREVIEW:

Introduction (Condensed)

Tim Tender was hired to resolve the disappearance and, later, murder of a notable author in the "case of the stolen manuscript."

He had learned some of his skills as a private investigator as far back as the days when he grew up in a small, west central town in Florida, called Saint Petersburg. He had, at the time, been a student at Lakeside Elementary in his sixth-grade, big-shot year.... Tim felt he had developed a knack and a love for solving things in those early days, which is why he decided to study in college about crime and how to unravel mysteries.

And, after reading the remarkable book, *The Big Sleep*, by the marvelous writer of detective fiction, Raymond Chandler, Tim Tender knew that *P.I.* was the title he eventually wanted next to his monogram....

...Philip Marlowe, the mythical private eye in Chandler's novels, along with, the great Sam Spade dreamt up by another fabulous *penman* of the hard-boiled story, Dashiell Hammett, became posters on the walls of Tim's young life--presiding in prominence on the plaster next to his *horror* favorites: Karloff, Lorre, and Price. The whole family of banners now adorned the walls of his one man/one woman office in the state of the famed Orioles.

Tim presently lives and works within a once sleepy city in Maryland—Laurel, a suburb between Baltimore and Washington, D.C., off the *BW Parkway*. It is much like his hometown in Florida, where people seem to prefer *laid-back*, a term that *slow* covered back during the Fifties in Timothy's Saint Petersburg.

185

But, now, the dead body of a famous resident that had lived on Silverbirch Lane in the exclusive Montpelier section of Laurel has turned up. And, what makes it a high profile case is that the corpse was the best-selling writer of horror classics, Jake Venom....

The movie, *Tender Nightmare*...hailed by the cinema- going public as scarier than Hitchcock's *Psycho*...was pulling in box office receipts previously unheard of. Jake had written the screenplay, which was based on *his* publication by the same title. The book had been his latest release, retailing five million copies, far outdistancing his prior prize winner, *The Ghost of Auguste Escoffier Tours The Carlton*, which sold just a *mil.* x two.

Tender Nightmare, the novel, had been Venom's only success in the last five years....

His latest story, *The Godfather of Bane*, never reached Jake's editor at Premature Burial Publishing. He was killed on the way to the post office. The manuscript turned up missing....

...Tim Tender was good at his craft; he had solved difficult cases, even as young as his business was, which is the reason Mrs. Venom, Vicki, had decided to employ the *Tender PI Company*—a one private eye/one office manager operation. Although Tim didn't proceed in the same aggressive, tough manner as the detectives, Marlowe and Spade, he was honest, as they were. He had inherited the easy-going style of his father. The P.I. found that it also made things easier with the cops he dealt with on a consistent basis....

But, people didn't need to be fooled by Tim's unassuming *modus operandi*. He was wiry, but it was six feet of solid wire, and he had taken involuntary boxing lessons at his high school alma mater, Lakehood Senior; therefore, he could "put his foot down" if necessary.

His colleague's logo was Bea E. Hopkins, a beautiful, competent, confident woman, and former Lakehood High star softball player. She had also lived in Saint Petersburg but was originally from Baltimore. Timothy and Bea were engaged to be married. They were a good team. When they stood face to face, he could kiss the top of her head that had dark, down-to-the-shoulder-blades, straight hair....

Timothy told me, his *dear* friend, this story as we were waiting out a severe ice storm at the Salvation Army shelter in Glen Burnie, MD. We still argue about which team plays the best *roundball*, the Celtics or the Bullets?

The tale may be hard to accept; but, then again, maybe it's not. You, the reader, need not know my name. Tim had studied criminal law at a university in a town north of Los Angeles and began his investigating career in the City of Angels....

The year that the master storyteller of terror, Jake Venom, was killed, average human life expectancy was 70.8 years.

Unfortunately, the cessation of foul play did not end with Jake Venom's well-attended, star-studded, dual cremation ceremonies: the first one at the Baltimore gravesite of the legendary author, Edgar Allan Poe, Venom's hero; the second, held at the one-time Maryland residence of the writer and poet, creator of one of Tim Tender's favorites, "The Fall of the House of Usher."

Chapter 1

Thursday, 3:00 p.m., 1970

"Hey, Rip, that Jake Venom, huh?" Tim Tender asked as he shook the *plainclothesman's* hand. From his Florida beach days, the private detective had inherited a constant tan and looked like a tall pretzel.

"That's him, P.I.," Lt. Ripken Omaha said. He released his hand from his friend's. The lieutenant looked like a drill sergeant: wide, muscular shoulders; short-cropped, silver-blond hair; and square jaw.

The officer reminded Tim of his own brother, his twin-in-past-mischievous-crime, Todd.

Omaha was a durable cop, discounting days-off and vacation periods, Ripken Omaha hadn't missed a day on the beat for 2,131 days in a row. Even had his nose busted by a D.U.I. collar in his early days on traffic cop duty—he still showed for work the next day.

Rip had broken another policeman's record for consecutive *keeping-the-peace* days—a man that had been a foot soldier in New York City, home of the dreaded Yankees. Officer Louis Henry, who, sadly, had died of *amyotrophic lateral sclerosis,* also known as Lou Gehrig's disease, had held the record of 2,130 between the years of 1925 and 1939.

Astonishing accomplishments in both cases.

Lieutenant Omaha presently worked out of Central District One, which covered urban areas like the Inner Harbor, Theatre District, the adult school-yard section called "The Block," district houses of Government—and many hotels and residences. The sector of Baltimore also drew millions of tourists each year, which made law enforcement even more difficult.

"Mrs. Venom hire you?" The Lt. pointed his right forefinger toward the P.I.

"Yes, after her husband turned up missing. Said he went to mail a manuscript and then to the Freedom Inn for some crab cake sandwiches; but, didn't come home. Kind of peculiar that he left on Monday but she didn't call me until Wednesday." The private eye held back, at the present time, information about the story being lost.

"The 'Rich.' Who can tell about their motives on living. Hey, the Freedom's got the best crab-on-bread, they use the most lump and backfin meat, the firmest lett..."

"Yes, I know; I've heard it all before." Tender's face showing sarcasm. "What's that tied to his right arm?"

"Believe it or not, it's a Webster's Dictionary. Here, use my pen to flip through these page numbers—1, 102, 167, 373, 718, 1506, 1517, and 1550. And be careful, it's a Paper Mate. The pages are a little ragged so it'll take some doing. Here's a pad, write down the words that are highlighted." Omaha didn't want his chum to corrupt any evidence at the crime scene.

Tim bent down and crossed under the yellow-and-black tape surrounding the crime scene. "I have my own notebook and pen, a Montblanc. What's with the *Caution: Wet Paint* on the strip surrounding the body?"

"All the *Police Line: Do Not Cross* ones are being used; Captain Calvert ordered more, but Chief Crossland said they haven't arrived. They come all the way from England, you know." Omaha pointed in a northeasterly direction that he thought would be where Europe was on the compass.

"No, I didn't."

"That's probably because you're from Florida and not Maryland." Ripken performed a 180-degree turn on his tiptoes like a ballerina and nodded his head southwesterly towards Saint Petersburg, the P.I.'s hometown.

"Busy day, huh?" Tim asked as if he already knew the answer.

"It's Thursday," the Lt. said matter-of-factly.

The phrase that Tender came up with from the dictionary was: *a bad boy deserved it was were you.* "What is that supposed to mean? Do we label it the 'Bad Grammar Killer Case'?"

"Shuffle the words." Omaha used a lot of poker and billiard terms when he spoke. Not Omaha Hold'em—an obvious choice—but Seven Stud was his favorite card game—usually won at it, too. But, Tim normally beat Ripken at pocket pool—they almost always played Nine Ball, with a rare Eight Ball game dropping the black ball in for the winner.

" 'You were a bad boy, it was deserved,' " P.I. Tender stated. "Revenge murder, huh? Any prints on the word book?"

"No, lab boys dusted. He's got a slug between his eyes, looks like it could've been a *hit*. Small cannon shot just like the round was caromed offa billiard ball."

"Think he was on the take with the Mob?"

"Wouldn't have thought it, but his nose," the Lt. rubbed beneath his own smeller, "area does look raw. Get a little closer, check out his mouth."

Tender moved a few feet forward and closed in on the dead body's now silent speaker section. "It's full of raw oysters!"

"Definitely a full-house."

"Are those blood stains on his shirt?"

"Cocktail sauce. Sergeant Small was able to get a small taste. Very little blood around the wound. Let's get outa here, the coroner's boys can handle everything else. I'll check with ballistics later to find out about the *pistola*, and with the M.E. to see if his death was actually caused by the tiny torpedo lodged in his head. I'm hungry, how 'bout Costa's Restaurant for some crabs and a ginger beer."

Omaha usually preferred a Krueger Beer with his crabs but only drank nonalcoholic stuff on duty; Tender, in his profession, didn't have such restrictions. But, he also wouldn't overdo while he was working a case, or driving. He enjoyed an orange soda with his *blues*, sometimes two.

Off-duty, Tim occasionally liked a Beefeater and Soda but could only drink it with ice and the juice of a chunk of lime squeezed into the mix. Never drank more than one at a time. Bea, Tim's beloved, liked a glass of dry red wine, *cabernet sauvignon*, especially, but lately it had been giving her headaches. Consequently, she had switched to an arid white, *Chardonnay*, preferring the grape of the French Vineyards to those of the Napa Valley.

"Let's take my ride, I'll drop you off later to get yours," the cop told the gumshoe. Omaha drove a 1958 Ford Edsel—three-tone job, different shades the same color as champagne. His was from the Citation series. He told Tim he wanted horsepower and tailfins; also, said that the salesman won him over with the automatic transmission controlled by push buttons in the center of the steering wheel. The car seller stated to Ripken that the Edsel would be "big"—a luxury model that would compete against the great ones from Buick, Oldsmobile, and the "New Yorker" from Chrysler. As popular as the car was supposed to become, the police detective felt he could get a newer model every three years and get a good trade-in value to boot.

"Told you this baby would be worth some money—you know I'm a charter member of the Edsel Owner's Club, signed on in '68."

"You're lucky it became a collector's item or bye-bye good investment," Tim said. "Now, talk about an instant legend, my 1965 Mustang, '289' powerhouse, could blow your doors out."

"That's *in*, not *out*. You're as dumb as a scratched cue ball."

"Minor detail, huh. The original 'Stang in '64, by its first birthday on April 17, 1965, sold over 400,000 cars, about 4 times the total Edsels that were made in the first 25 months on the market." Tender's vehicle was black with a white convertible top; his dad had bought it for him as a graduation present, after his youngest twin completed his Criminal Justice degree at Fresno State in

California. Tim told me (the Celtic fan, remember?) that Dad Tender had clued him in that the vehicle would be special. P.I. Tender was also restoring a '57 Thunderbird Roadster, which still had the original Volumatic Radio System that would increase the tune player's loudness as the automobile accelerated. The "312" cubic-inch engine with dual four-barrel *venturi* carburetors cranked out "270 horses." Tim had bought it *for a song*—needed body work and a new paint job.

Omaha was looking for a 1954 T-Bird, one of the first to come off the assembly line at Dearborn, Michigan.

Classic cars was another reason the two justice seekers got along famously.

"Tim said: "Yes, Costa's sounds great, I can play some Keno."

The two friends headed toward the crab house for some eats, drinks, and gambling—innocent fun.

About the Author

RAY. E. SPENCER was born and raised in Saint Petersburg, Florida. He graduated with an English degree from the University of South Florida, Tampa campus. Ray lives with his wife, Bonnie, in Largo, Florida. He is employed by the LIMO, Inc.

Ray has completed a screenplay, *The Stolen Manuscript: The Dictionary Murders (a mystery in the Tim Tender series),* and is currently in the final rewrite of a novel by the same title. He is also working on a screenplay for *Tender Nightmare.*